Face To Face

Face To Face
© 2008 by Melanie L. Wilber
Revised and Updated, 2014
All Rights Reserved

This is a work of fiction. The characters, incidents, and dialogues are products of the author's imagination. Except for well-known historical and contemporary figures, any resemblance to actual events or persons is entirely coincidental.

Dedication

For you, dear reader
May you see Him face to face

For now we see in a mirror dimly,
but then face to face.

1 Corinthians 13:12

Chapter One

Brianne was so excited. She had been to camp earlier this summer with Austin, Sarah, and her family, but she was looking forward to a great week as a middle school camper. This was the last week of the summer she had any plans, and the week she had been looking forward to more than any other.

She had gone to camp many times before, but this was the first time she was going with so many friends. She wasn't going to be in the same cabin with all of them. For one thing because several of her friends were boys, and for another because the camp had a limit of four friends being together in the same cabin, and there were ten girls altogether in their group.

Sarah and Briana were going. Briana was a friend from Sarah's school in Portland. Brianne had met her when she had spent a week with Sarah at her house three weeks ago, and Brianne really liked her. She was different than Sarah, more quiet and shy, but she was nice and fun to be around.

Emily, Brooke, and Marissa were also going. Marissa had invited her friend Kayla to come, and her own cousin from Washington, Justine, was coming too. She had seen her for a few days this week when she had been in

Bellingham with her family. Justine had come back with them yesterday so she could ride down to camp today.

Ashlee and Caitlin were going also. Brianne had mixed feelings, but she was trying to remain positive about having them along. She had been praying for Ashlee for several months, and in recent weeks she seemed to be heading in a good direction. Brianne knew Caitlin would be exposed to hearing about God's love for her, and she was praying for a good week for them, but having them along would create some amount of anxiety. She was trying not to think about it too much.

She wasn't sure whom she would be in the same cabin with. When she had originally signed up in the spring, she had listed Sarah, Emily, and Marissa as her preferred cabin mates. Brooke had listed her, Emily, and Marissa, hoping the five of them could be together instead of only four. But then Sarah had invited Briana. Marissa had invited Kayla. And Justine had decided to come. She hoped all eight of them could be together, but she wasn't getting her heart set on it. As long as she was with one of her other friends and none of them were alone, she would be happy, although she really hoped she and Sarah could be together because she wouldn't be seeing her again after this week.

They had ten guys going along this year too, including Austin, Michael, Tim, Jason, Sarah's ex-boyfriend, Ryan, Austin's younger brother, Calvin, her own younger brother J.T., and his best friend from school. They were only sixth graders, but Pastor Doug had decided to bring sixth graders into youth group this year, and the camp included them as a part of middle school camp also.

Brianne was in the shower, imagining what this week would be like, when she realized she'd better get out before she used up all the hot water and there wasn't any left for her cousin. Justine had still been sleeping when she got out of bed, but she needed to wake her soon if they were going to get out of here on time. Pastor Doug and his new assistants, Josh and Anna, were driving everyone down today, and they were supposed to be meeting at the church at ten.

Her dad was officially on vacation until Monday, so they weren't going to church this morning as a family, which felt really strange. Even when they had been in Bellingham, they'd gone to church with her grandparents. She was still thinking about that too. Last Sunday she went to the youth class on Sunday morning and had been invited to go on a day-trip to the Northwest Washington Fair with them on Wednesday. She and Justine went together, and Brianne had spent about an hour alone with one of the guys in the youth group.

They hadn't planned it. She had every intention of spending the entire day with Justine, along with Katie and Katie's friends. And she did for most of the day. But at three o'clock they were all supposed to meet by the Ferris wheel to check in with the youth leaders, and after they did, Brianne needed to use the restroom along with the other girls, so they found one together. She had stepped out of the restroom first and was waiting for Justine and the others when Alex saw her and came over to talk.

She hadn't realized it before, but Alex was the pastor's son. Someone had mentioned it on the drive there, and when he was talking to her she mentioned it. They talked for several minutes, and she totally missed Justine and Katie and the other girls coming out of the restroom. When she realized it, she and Alex walked around the immediate area looking for them, but they were nowhere to be found.

She had remembered Katie saying something about wanting to go on the Ferris wheel, so they wandered back over that way and wondered if the girls were already on the ride. She and Alex waited until the current riders got off, but their friends weren't among them. Then Alex asked if she wanted to go for a ride with him, and she accepted the invitation because she had no idea where everyone else had disappeared to, and she liked talking to Alex.

After their ride on the Ferris wheel, they had wandered around together looking for others in their group but had also played carnival games and ridden a couple of other rides together. She'd had a lot of fun and hadn't felt awkward about being alone with him until they finally ran into Katie and her friends again, and then Justine made a big deal about them "sneaking off together", which wasn't true, but by the time they were headed back to Bellingham after the evening concert, everyone was convinced it was.

She liked Justine, and she was glad she was coming to camp with her, but sometimes she could be—well, a brat, and Brianne had been sort of mad at her over it. As far as Alex was concerned, she wasn't interested in being his girlfriend any more than any of the guys she had in her own youth group, but she did think he was nice and she'd had fun with him. She didn't like the way Justine had turned their time together into something it wasn't, and she really hoped her cousin didn't mention any of it to her friends today, but she had the feeling she would.

"Brianne, are you about done in there?" her mom said on the other side of the door as she dried herself off. "Justine wants to use the shower too."

"Yeah, I'll be out in a minute," she called out. "What time is it?"

"Nine-fifteen."

"Sorry. I'm almost done," she said, feeling surprised it was that late. She dressed as quickly as possible, brushed out her hair, and took her hairdryer to her room, telling Justine the shower was free.

Her cousin acted annoyed she'd had to wait so long, and once she left the room, Brianne had the feeling it was going to be more of a challenge being at camp with her than she had anticipated. But still, she was excited about going, and she was especially excited about seeing her friends she had been away from these last two weeks.

Finishing her packing, drying her hair, and taking her things to the van, she tried to ignore Justine's grumpy mood and be happy. When they arrived at the church, Justine seemed in better spirits, but Brianne knew she was nervous about meeting a bunch of people she didn't know. Justine had self-esteem issues she struggled with a lot. Her twin sister, Jenna, was taller, skinnier, and more social than she was. And even though Justine had gotten help for the eating-disorder she had fallen into last year, Brianne had seen her insecurity and dissatisfaction with herself surfacing in other ways this week.

She exaggerated about everything to the point of lying at times, but Brianne hadn't called her on it. Not yet, anyway. She had decided if Justine tried to make more of what had happened between her and Alex in front of her friends here, she would talk to her and ask her to stop. She'd almost said something last night but had decided to wait and see if it became an issue.

She also tended to talk poorly about other people, pointing out all of their faults and things she didn't like about them. Several times when they had gone to the fair, Justine had been talking to someone sweetly one moment, and then five minutes later she was talking badly behind their back. Brianne said something about it a couple of times, but it didn't seem to make much difference. Justine would say, 'Well, it's true. I'm just stating a fact.' And often it was, but Brianne didn't think it was a nice thing to say and wished she would keep her thoughts to herself.

Getting out of the van at the church, Brianne saw most of the others were already here. They would be picking up Sarah, Briana, and Ryan in Portland on their way to the camp. She saw Austin helping load one of the large vans Pastor Doug had rented for the trip and felt like running over to say 'hi' and give him a hug, but she didn't. She would be seeing him soon, and she had told herself on the way here to include Justine and help her get to know the other girls, not abandon her.

They both carried some of their things over to one of the vans, and her dad followed behind with the rest. J.T. and his friend only had one bag each plus their sleeping bags, so they carried their own. When she first heard her brother was going to camp with her, she had been a little annoyed, but after thinking about it she was glad he was going along with the guys her age rather than with the other sixth and seventh grade boys who had gone to camp two weeks ago while they had been on vacation. She knew Austin and Calvin were good influences on J.T., and Joel, Silas, and Ryan would be too.

She looked around for Silas but didn't see him. He'd gone to New Mexico with his family on vacation, and she hadn't seen him for three weeks, the day before she had gone to visit Sarah in Portland.

"Looking for me?" she heard someone whisper in her ear while she was scanning the parking area. Turning around, she saw Austin standing six inches away, and she smiled.

"Actually, I was looking for Silas," she teased him. "Is he here yet?"

"Not yet," he laughed, shaking his head at her exaggerated excitement about seeing his "competition" more so than him. "Good to see you too, Brianne."

They both knew she was teasing, and she stepped forward, giving him a heartfelt hug. She talked to him on the phone once this week, but she had missed him terribly. Especially since Wednesday when she had been made to feel like there was something wrong with hanging out with a boy as a friend. She had grown so used to it with Austin she hadn't thought about her time with Alex until Justine made a big deal out of it.

She hadn't been feeling this way before now, but she suddenly wished it would be just her, Austin, and Sarah going to camp together, meeting Joel there, and having the kind of times they'd had together last month.

"I missed you," she whispered.

"I missed you too," Austin replied.

She had a brief moment to enjoy a connection with him before it was rudely interrupted.

"Uh-oh," Brianne heard Justine say behind her, and she knew what was coming. "Does Alex know about this guy, Brianne? Should I call him and say he's got competition and better get his cute self down here?"

Brianne had been praying all morning she could handle this moment when it came, and God gave her the perfect words to silence her cousin—and make Austin smile.

"Tell Alex it's too late. I already have a best friend. I don't need him too."

Chapter Two

Austin needed to help his dad load the vans and said he would see her later. After he stepped away, Brianne said 'hi' to her other friends and introduced them all to Justine, who didn't say anything else for the moment about Austin or any of the guys who were here.

Brianne had the chance to meet Josh and Anna, and she liked both of them instantly. They were in their early twenties and were going to be helping with the youth group from now on. Josh and Anna had moved back to Clatskanie after being away at college and then living in Portland for a couple of years. They were getting married next month and seemed excited about meeting her and all of them. Apparently they'd been at church last Sunday when she had been gone, so some of the others had already met them, but not everyone.

Marissa hadn't because she had been out of town, and neither had Brooke because she didn't come to their church except on Thursday nights when Brianne was there too. Anna was friendly and sweet, and Brianne had forgotten about them being here and going to camp with them until this morning, so her presence boosted her mood after Justine had dampened it. She learned Anna and Josh had both worked at the camp as counselors, and when Anna said her camp name, Brianne recognized her from when she had been a camper there a few years ago.

"I had Jelly Bean as my counselor, and you were right next door. Our cabins slept outside together."

"Ah, Jelly Bean," Anna smiled. "I haven't seen her in forever. I'll have to try and call her this week and see if she can come down for a day. We were best friends that summer."

Pastor Doug began to gather everyone together so they could say a group prayer before they loaded up the vans. Brianne and the others followed his instructions, but as she walked over to the large circle he was forming, Anna walked beside her and said something to her privately.

"I've heard a lot about you from Pastor Doug. I'm looking forward to getting to know you this week."

"I've heard a lot about you too, and Janie. Did she move here with you and Josh?"

Anna smiled. "Yes. And she's happy about it. It's been a long road, but this has taught me something about never giving up on people when God is involved."

As they stepped into the circle and waited for Pastor Doug to pray, Brianne thought of several people she needed to hang in there with and not give up on. Her cousin, for one, along with Ashlee and Caitlin. Maybe this week she would see some of those prayers answered, and she decided to remain optimistic until she had a reason to feel discouraged about any of them.

Her thoughts were challenged five minutes later when Justine said something to her about Austin. They had taken seats in the same van they had put their stuff in. Brooke, Marissa, and Kayla were behind them, Ashlee and Caitlin were in the back, and they were saving three seats in front for Sarah, Briana, and Ryan.

"Why didn't you tell me you had a boyfriend here?" Justine whispered. "I wouldn't have made a big deal about you and Alex if I had known."

"Austin's not my boyfriend," she said. "He's my best friend."

"Same thing," she said.

"No, it's not. We're friends, not boyfriend and girlfriend."

Justine didn't appear convinced, but Brianne wasn't going to argue with her. She was about to change the subject and ask her about something else when Austin was suddenly at her side, occupying the empty space beside her and appearing as though he was planning to stay.

"What are you doing? I thought you were riding in the 'boys-only" van?" she said, as it had been named five minutes ago by Tim and Jason.

"Too much male-bonding for me," he said. "I'll keep you girls company. You have plenty of room until we pick up the other three."

"You could sit up there," she said, pointing to the completely empty seat in front of them. "You would have it all to yourself for an hour."

He smiled at her. "No, thanks. I'm fine right here."

"Well, since you're here, can you please tell my cousin you are not my boyfriend? She doesn't believe me."

Austin leaned forward to look at Justine on her other side. "I'm not her boyfriend. I'm her best friend—well, until Sarah's here, and then I'm her second best friend."

He sat back as if that settled it, and Justine didn't say anything else, but Brianne knew she would hear more about her cousin's opinion later. For now she changed the subject, and the three of them talked for the next hour before they reached Portland and met up with Sarah and her friends where they were stopping for lunch.

Once Sarah, Briana, and Ryan were in the van too, their talking and laughter only increased. Austin decided to remain sitting beside her instead of going back to his van, and when they reached the camp at two o'clock, Brianne's loneliness of missing her friends was well in the past. Much to their delight, all of the girls ended up in the same cabin, except for Caitlin and Ashlee who had only requested each other on their registration forms. They seemed perfectly fine with that and separated from them at the bottom of the girls' cabin area to go find theirs at the top of the hill. The one the rest of them had been assigned to was just across from the bathrooms in the lower portion of the cabin area, and they invaded their overwhelmed-looking counselor within thirty seconds. She was sweet though, and Brianne promised her they wouldn't be too rowdy.

"I'm sure we'll have lots of fun together," Kit Kat said. "Just give me a couple of hours to get all your names straight."

Brianne was anxious to see Joel, but she decided not to mention that to Justine and go running off to try and find him, or her cousin would get the wrong idea about him too. She would be seeing him soon enough anyway. It wasn't that big of a camp, and she knew Joel would be looking for her at dinner if she didn't see him sooner.

Once they had gotten settled in their cabin, Marissa said something about a cute guy they had seen when they first arrived, and she and Kayla decided to look for him. Brianne knew Marissa was probably doing it more so for Kayla. She wasn't that way about guys usually, and she had a little something going with Pete back home anyway. They weren't officially together, and Marissa had told him she wasn't ready, but they had spent some time together these last few weeks. Marissa had said something to her earlier and sounded favorable about it. Brianne was hoping for a chance to talk to her more later.

Brooke and Emily decided to go along too, and when they asked her and Justine if they wanted to go, Justine said 'yes', but Brianne said she would stay here. Sarah and Briana had already decided the same, and it was the first time Justine left her side. Brianne laid down on her bunk and let out a pent-up sigh once the others were gone.

"What's that about?" Sarah asked. She and Briana had sat down to give each other manicures.

"Nothing," she said, choosing not to talk about her cousin behind her back. "It's good to be here. I've been waiting all summer for this."

"I know," Sarah said. "Me too."

The cabins held ten girls in all, and two others came in a few minutes later, met Kit Kat, and took the remaining two bunks. Sarah introduced herself to them along with Briana. Brianne told them her name also, and they seemed nice. Neither of them had been here before so they left to explore the camp. Brianne enjoyed the peacefulness of the cabin and listened to Briana and Sarah talking but didn't talk much herself. She felt tired from the long morning and Justine's often-annoying chatter and attitude.

She fell asleep and woke when Kit Kat told her it was time to head to dinner. She rubbed her eyes and rolled over, seeing she was the only one in the cabin besides her counselor.

"I guess I *was* tired," she said, recalling her earlier words. She had meant it more in an emotional sense, but she had been physically tired too, she supposed.

"Were you too excited to sleep last night?" Kit Kat asked, sounding like she knew what that was like.

"Yes, and we got back late," she said, checking herself in the mirror quickly.

"Where were you?"

Brianne told her about being in Washington with her family for two weeks, and she shared a bunch of other stuff as they walked to the lake where a barbecue was being held for dinner.

"I thought you looked familiar," Kit Kat said when she mentioned being here during Primary Camp as a junior counselor. "So you know the Wests?"

"Yes. We used to live in Sweet Home, and my dad was the pastor of the church they go to. Megan was my counselor last year, and I was her JC a few weeks ago. And I know Joel really well. He's one of my best friends."

They got plates and began to go through the line. She had put ketchup on her hamburger bun when she felt a tap on her shoulder. Turning around, she saw Joel standing there, and she smiled.

"You made it," he said. "I was beginning to wonder after not seeing you all afternoon."

"I took a nap," she said.

"A nap? On the first day of camp?"

"I know," she laughed. "That's so not me."

"Hi, Brianne," she heard someone else say, and she turned to see Anna and Josh going through the line across the table from her.

"Hi," she said. "This is my friend, Joel—Oh, you probably already know him."

"Joel?" Anna said, obviously knowing who she meant but not recognizing him at this age and height. "You were like ten the last time I was here! What happened?"

"Got a little taller, Froot Loop," he said, giving her his best smile.

Brianne bragged on him then, telling Anna and Josh about the lookout tower he was building. Joel invited them to come see it sometime, and they said they would. Before he stepped away to get his own food, he whispered something in her ear.

"Can you meet me there in thirty minutes?"

"Okay," she said.

"Joel's sweet," Kit Kat commented after he stepped away. "He's always helping out in the kitchen. Is he a camper this week, or was he coming over to say hi to you?"

"He's a camper. We planned to be here the same week. Last year he was gone on a rafting trip with his youth group, and it was a major bummer."

She filled up her plate with the remaining items and looked around for her friends, seeing most of them sitting together on the grassy hillside surrounding the lake. She and Kit Kat went to join them, and Brianne was glad to see Justine had struck up a friendship with Emily and Brooke. They all knew she had taken a nap because they'd been at the cabin after she fell asleep but left again before she woke up.

As they ate, Brianne wondered how she was going to get away to meet Joel without telling the others. If Justine wasn't here, she would feel comfortable being honest about it. Her other friends knew about Joel and how they'd grown up together. They sometimes teased her about seeing him whenever they came here, but they didn't go overboard like Justine had about Alex.

The perfect opportunity presented itself when they were finished eating. Megan spotted her and came over to say 'hi' and give her a hug. They talked for a few minutes casually, and then Brianne asked if she could go for a walk around the lake with her, hinting she had something she wanted to talk to her about.

"Sure," Megan said.

"You don't have to wait for me," she told Kit Kat and the others who were right around her. "I'll catch up later."

Once she was alone with Megan, she told her about needing to meet Joel in five minutes, but that wasn't the only reason she had pulled Megan away. She really did want to ask her something.

"What do you do when God is telling you to be around someone you don't like much?"

"Anyone I know?" Megan asked.

"No, it's my cousin. She's here this week, and I'm the one who invited her to come. But she's driving me crazy!"

Megan laughed. "It's only the first day."

"I've been around her since Tuesday, and by Wednesday I was totally ticked-off at her. What am I going to do?" she whined, falling into Megan's shoulder.

"Why were you mad at her?"

Brianne told her the story about Alex at the Fair. Megan listened and said something Brianne didn't expect her to say.

"I can't believe how much you've grown up since last summer."

"What do you mean?"

"A year ago, you would have seen hanging around with Alex much differently, Brianne. Admit it."

Brianne honestly hadn't thought of that, but she could see what Megan meant. Last summer she and Sarah had gone boy-crazy over one guy Megan had heard about all week, and they hadn't even talked to him except for five minutes one afternoon when they were waiting in line at the Snack Shack.

"Okay, I admit it," she said. "I keep forgetting how much different this year turned out than I was expecting."

"And how did it turn out? I haven't gotten a letter in awhile, and we didn't have a chance to talk when you were here last month."

She had told Megan about Austin becoming her best friend, but she hadn't shared the whole truth with her. "You know why I didn't consider spending time with Alex as any big deal, besides the fact I've learned how to see guys as friends for now?"

"Why?"

"Because if I'm not ready to go there with Austin or Joel yet, then I know I'm not ready to go there with some guy I hadn't spent any time with until this week. We had fun together, but not anything like when I'm with two of my best friends."

"Try to keep in mind Justine hasn't experienced that yet. When she has, then she'll understand, but right now, she can't."

"Yeah, you're right, and to you I probably seem immature even now, huh?" She laughed.

"I don't know about that. You're different than you were last summer. I noticed when you were here before, and I could hear a difference in your letters too. That last one where you were talking about enjoying your relationship with God and not getting caught up in wondering if you're being good enough or doing enough stuff for Him? That challenged me!"

"It did?"

"Yes! I had to take a step back and say, 'Am I doing that?' And I knew I was. I came into this summer thinking a lot differently about my relationship with Him and what I'm doing here than I ever have before. So, whatever you're doing to grow closer to Jesus and see Him the way we all should, don't stop, Brianne. Don't stop."

Chapter Three

When Brianne and Megan arrived at the base of the lookout tower, Joel was there waiting. Megan needed to go, and she left them alone, saying she hoped to see her later. Brianne gave Joel a hug and asked what was up. He answered by going to the ladder and asking her to follow him. She did, and when they got to the landing of the lower deck, he made an announcement.

"It's finished."

"It is? Everything? Even the upstairs?"

"Yep. And I wanted you to be the first to see it."

She took a look around and could see the finishing touches on the railing and built-in bench on the far end of the deck. He led her upstairs, and she saw the window frames were complete along with the benches lining the entire area. She sat down on one of them, looked up at him, and smiled. It was perfect.

"You're amazing," she said. "I can't believe you made this! I couldn't make a birdhouse if I tried."

He came to sit beside her, and he seemed proud of himself. "I can't believe I made it either. But once I got started, I couldn't stop. And I looked forward to the day I could sit up here and enjoy it."

"With me?" she asked.

He smiled. "With you. By myself. It's peaceful, you know?"

They sat in silence for a moment. She could hear a bird chirping, and the wind was gently coming through the open windows and rustling the tree branches surrounding the tower.

"You're not mad at me, are you?" he said.

She adjusted her position to sit sideways on the bench and face him. "No. Why would you think that?"

"You haven't written to me since the last letter I wrote to you."

"I've been busy," she replied. "I started one when we were at my grandparents', but I got interrupted and never finished."

"What did you say?"

"I don't remember. Nothing important."

He didn't say anything, and she decided to be totally honest.

"I wanted to respond to what you said, but I wasn't sure what to say. I feel like I already told you how I felt when I was here."

"But you didn't know I was thinking about kissing you."

"No, but I was thinking I wanted you to."

He got an adorable smile on his face. "You were?"

She laughed. "Yes. And I'd never felt that way before. I couldn't believe it when I read you had been thinking the same thing."

He held her gaze, and she didn't look away.

"I don't want to now," he said. "I mean I do, but I meant what I said, and I know this isn't the right time. I don't want you to avoid me this week or be worried I'm going to kiss you one day, because I won't."

She smiled and inwardly relaxed. She hadn't been worried about it, but the thought had crossed her mind, especially thirty minutes ago when he told her he wanted to meet her here.

"I want us to have a super-fun week," she said. "And I want some time with you every day; either just us, or you, me, Austin, Sarah, and whoever else wants to tag along, okay?"

"Okay. When tomorrow?"

"How about swimming after lunch?"

"Sounds good. Can I take you on a canoe ride?"

"Sure. I'd love that."

She told him who all was here, and she asked him to pray about her time with Justine. She didn't go into details, but she said one thing that applied specifically to him.

"If you hear her saying anything about a guy named Alex, or Austin being my boyfriend, or you, just ignore her, okay? She thinks any guy I talk to for more than five minutes must be my boyfriend."

"Who's Alex?" he asked.

She laughed. "Never mind. A guy I know in Washington. Come on, we'd better get back," she said, rising from the bench.

He followed her, and once they were on the ground, they walked together to where the trail to the guys' cabins veered off the main path. They both needed to change into warmer clothes for the evening activities.

"Who's your counselor?" she asked him.

"Shark. Who's yours?"

"Kit Kat."

"That's Shark's sister."

"Oh yeah? I didn't know that."

"Yep."

Brianne could remember when she used to know all the ins and outs of the summer staff members when she lived here and hung out with Joel a lot. She knew who was related to whom, which staff members were dating each other, and they all knew her and Joel, calling them "camp rats". She missed those days.

"Kit Kat said you help in the kitchen a lot."

"Yeah. I like it."

"Are any of your friends from church here with you this week?"

"No, they were here a few weeks ago."

"I'm sorry. That's probably a bummer."

"Not really," he said. "You're here."

"I know, but I can't be in the same cabin with you. You have to make all new friends this week."

"Not all," he said. "Austin is in my cabin."

"He is!" She laughed. "You didn't tell me that. Who is Austin with? Michael?"

"Michael, Silas, and Ryan."

She laughed again. "That's too funny, or did you plan that?"

"When you and Austin were here last month, Austin asked me if I was coming with other friends, and when I told him no, he said, 'If there's any way you can get yourself into our cabin, then do it.'"

Austin hadn't mentioned that to her. She could understand Austin wanting to hang out with Joel this week. They'd had a great time last month, but why wouldn't he tell her? When she saw Austin twenty minutes later, he was with Joel and their other cabin mates. They had all arrived for the Sunday Night Show being held in the large barn on the other side of the lake, a traditional beginning to the start of any camp week. Austin didn't seem to make any special note of the fact Joel was with them when she went over to say a brief hello, nor later when they were all leaving the evening program to go back to their cabins and prepare for lights-out.

"Where were you earlier?" Austin asked.

"When?"

"All afternoon? After dinner?"

"I took a nap when we got here, and I spent time with Joel after dinner. Why didn't you tell me you had invited him to be in your cabin?"

He shrugged. "I thought I did."

"No, I don't think so."

"What's wrong with that?"

"Nothing. That was nice of you. I'm just wondering why you didn't say anything."

"This way I can keep my eye on him," he teased her.

"That's what I figured," she laughed, but she didn't think he was serious.

"Or maybe he can keep an eye on me."

She thought that might be more truthful. "Really?"

"No," he said. "I just like the guy. I admit it. He's too nice to not like, even if he is my strongest competition right now. If we're going to be here together all summer in three years, I figure I may as well get used to it."

Austin and Joel were different in a lot of ways, but she could picture them becoming good friends. Even best friends if they lived in the same place and went to the same church and school, or spent an entire summer together.

"We're going swimming tomorrow after lunch," she said. "You're invited too."

"Okay," he said. "Can I get a canoe ride sometime?"

She laughed.

"What?"

She didn't answer.

"Joel already asked you?"

"Yes," she admitted.

"Okay, I get Tuesday then."

She laughed and linked her arm with his. She had missed him so much these last few weeks. Joel was walking a few paces ahead of them with Silas and Ryan, and she jogged to catch up with them, pulling Austin along with her. Linking her arm with Joel too, she walked with them until she had to say good-night.

Walking the rest of the way to her cabin with Sarah and Briana, she saw Justine, Brooke, and Emily had already arrived and were gathering their stuff to head to the bathrooms before bed. Justine and Emily left, and Brooke waited for her.

"Are you having fun so far?" she asked Brooke. She hadn't spent much time with her yet because she had taken that nap and then met with Joel after dinner.

"Yeah, it's fun," she said. "I'm glad we're all in the same cabin."

"Yeah, me too. Thanks for being nice to Justine. She would be thoroughly bored by now if it was up to me."

"Where were you after dinner?"

"I was talking to Joel. He showed me his lookout tower. It's all finished."

"Cool. Do we get to see it this time?"

"Sure. We can go there tomorrow."

Once they were in the bathroom, Brianne brushed her teeth, washed her face, and walked back with Emily, Justine, and Brooke when they were ready to go. Justine asked her where she had been after dinner, and she told her.

"Told you so," Emily said.

"Did he kiss you?" Justine asked.

Brianne hadn't told anyone about what Joel had written in his letter. Not even Sarah. "No. Why would you think that?"

"Emily said Austin isn't your boyfriend because you like Joel better."

"No, I don't. I like them the same. I'm friends with both of them."

Brianne didn't let Justine's words bother her after what Megan had said. She let it go and supposed the only way to convince Justine she didn't have a boyfriend was to let her see it for herself this week. And it didn't matter what her cousin thought anyway as long as Austin and Joel knew the truth.

After the lights had been turned out and they were supposed to be going to sleep, Brianne thought about the time she had spent with both Joel and Austin today. Since she'd had that nap earlier, she wasn't tired and prayed she could find the balance between her friendships this week. She also prayed for Ashlee and Caitlin, for them to have a good week and for their hearts to be open to what God wanted to teach them.

She prayed that for herself also, along with all of her friends. She knew last summer had been a spiritual turning-point for Austin, and she prayed the same would be true for whoever in their group needed that this summer.

Monday was a typical camp day, and she had a lot of fun. Most of them went swimming together after lunch, and she went on a canoe ride with Joel before heading back to the cabin to change and see what the rest of her friends had planned for the afternoon.

Stepping into the cabin, she saw Emily, Brooke, and Justine there, and they were the only ones. They seemed to stop talking suddenly when she entered the room. She asked where everyone was, and they said Sarah and Briana had gone to the camp store, Marissa and Kayla were taking showers, and the other two girls who were in the cabin with them had gone horseback riding.

Brianne decided she could use a shower too, and she knew from experience her chances of getting a hot one were better at this time of day than in the morning. She asked them what they were planning to do and where she might find them later if they left before she got back, and they said they were thinking of going to the craft shop to make bracelets.

"Okay, I'll meet you there if you want to go on ahead."

She left the cabin with a fresh change of clothes and her bag with her shampoo and stuff in it. She was almost to the shower house when she remembered she would need a towel too, and she returned to the cabin to get one. As she approached the cabin, she could hear the other girls talking through the open window close to the door. Thinking she heard one of them say her name, and in light of how they had acted when she'd returned earlier, she stopped before going up the steps, and she listened.

"She's being so flirty with every guy here," she heard Justine say. "She thinks my sister was bad for having a boyfriend my parents didn't know about, but she's got like five! How is that any better?"

"I know," Emily said. "She's the same way back home. I'm getting so sick of it. I feel like saying, 'Who are you dating this week, Brianne? Austin? Silas? Michael?' I'm like, 'Get over yourself, already. Let the rest of us have a chance.'"

She didn't hear Brooke say anything, but she didn't hear her defending her either. Slowly backing away from the cabin, she turned around and walked slowly to the shower house, feeling hurt and numb. To hear Justine or Ashlee talking behind her back would be one thing, but Emily? Brooke? They were her friends. And it hurt to think they saw her that way.

"Hi, Brianne," Marissa said when she entered the shower area.

"Hi," she said. Marissa and Kayla appeared to be about done. "Can I borrow your towel? I forgot mine."

"Sure," Marissa said, handing it to her. "How was your canoe ride?" She asked it sweetly, not like she was teasing her about being with Joel or accusing her of anything.

"It was fun. Time with Joel always is."

"He's so sweet," she said. "Are you going to take us to see his lookout tower later?"

"Sure. If you're in the cabin when I get back, we can go then. Or later if you have something else you want to do now."

"Not really," Marissa said. "We'll wait for you."

"Okay."

After they were gone, she wondered if when Marissa and Kayla got back to the cabin they would join in with the other girls talking about her. She didn't want to believe that about Marissa, but she couldn't believe it about Emily and Brooke either.

Once she was in the shower, she replayed Emily's words over in her mind and let the tears come. Suddenly she didn't want to be here at all. She wanted to go home.

Chapter Four

When Brianne returned to the cabin, Marissa and Kayla were there waiting for her, along with Sarah and Briana who had bought some things at the store. Sarah had gotten a shirt Brianne thought she would like to get for herself. It had a daisy on the front along with the words, "He loves me."

She knew it was referring to God, but she supposed if she got one and wore it, Justine might say, 'Who loves you today? Austin? Joel? Silas?'

She tried to hide her depressed feelings and decided she wouldn't say anything about going to the lookout tower until someone else mentioned it. Once she had put her stuff away, Marissa did, and Sarah and Briana said they wanted to go too, so they all left together. They stopped to get ice cream and other frozen treats at the Snack Shack and then she led the way. Walking up to the lake and past the swimming area, they saw Kit Kat, and she wondered where they were off to.

"I'm going to show them Joel's lookout tower," she said. "Have you seen it?"

"No, not yet. Can I come?"

"Sure," she said.

The excursion to the lookout tower lifted her spirits. Sarah and Marissa seemed to be treating her the same as always, and no one tried to make her and Joel's relationship into something it wasn't, even when Sarah told the rest of the girls what Joel had said last month about making it for her. They all thought that was sweet.

On the way back, Marissa and Kayla decided to stop by the boat dock for a canoe ride, and she went on ahead with Kit Kat, Sarah, and Briana back to the cabin. Kit Kat wanted to change out of her bathing suit, and Sarah and Briana wanted to write letters. Kit Kat asked them lots of questions about themselves, and it reminded Brianne of when they had been here last year and Megan had done the same thing. But it also reminded her how much things had changed in her life, which she thought had been for the better, but Emily's words had shaken her confidence. Maybe Emily and Justine were right about her being too flirty with guys and thinking she could have them as friends when she really couldn't.

She didn't see Justine, Emily, or Brooke until dinner, and she sat with them along with Sarah, Briana, Marissa, and Kayla. They sat at Megan's table and when Marissa mentioned going to the lookout tower, neither Emily nor Justine said anything about Joel, but she knew they were thinking it. She saw them exchange a look, and Justine rolled her eyes.

After dinner they had free time before the evening meeting, and they were hanging out on the back deck of the dining hall when the guys found them and came to sit with them too. Austin talked to her, but she didn't talk back to him in her usual way. She just answered his questions and tried her best to not be 'flirty' with him or any of the other guys.

They sat near them in the meeting, along with Josh and Anna who were there too. Brianne enjoyed the music, but she didn't feel like she could get into it, and the speaker was good, but what he had to say she already knew. She prayed silently near the end, asking God to help her through the rest of the day. She thought she had been doing a good job of following Him through all this complicated boy-stuff, but maybe she wasn't. She felt confused and alone.

After the meeting they had recreation time in the big field where they played relay-type games as cabin groups. They were dismissed shortly before sunset and were supposed to put on warmer clothing and meet at the campfire area. On the walk toward the cabins, Austin caught up with her, and he was by himself. She was with the girls in her cabin, but he tugged on her arm a bit and seemed to have something to say, so she fell back to walk with him.

"Are you okay?" he asked.

She didn't look at him, but she knew that was a mistake. He would know something was wrong for sure, so she looked at him but the concerned look on his face made her give it away anyway.

"What's going on?" he asked.

She didn't answer him. There were too many people around, and she didn't think she could say it. He pulled her off the main path to where a trail went down to the lake. It made her feel like she was sneaking off with him and doing something wrong, even though she wasn't.

"Austin! I need to go change."

"Brianne? No keeping secrets from me. Best friends don't do that, remember?"

She smiled a little. She was usually the one to say that, and she wanted to tell him, but she didn't know how. "Let's just say my cousin said one too many things about me having a bunch of boyfriends."

"What did she say?"

"It doesn't matter."

"It matters if you're this upset. You're never like this. What did she say?"

Brianne knew he was right. She had never felt this way before, and Austin was giving her a chance to talk about it. Relaying the conversation she had overheard earlier word-for-word, she held back the tears out of sheer willpower.

"Come here," Austin said, pulling her close to him and letting her cry. It was the first time she had cried about it besides in the shower, but crying with someone felt different than crying alone. And crying with Austin made her feel very close to him, reminding her he was her best friend and she hated having to put that aside like she had been doing all evening.

"You know how Emily can be sometimes," Austin said. "I've heard her do that before with other people, exaggerating the truth to go along with what someone else says."

"I know," she said. "It just hurts."

"Don't let it bother you. It's not true."

"It's not? Are you sure?" she asked seriously, stepping back to look at him.

"Not unless you've been kissing me and I don't remember, or you've been kissing Joel and Michael and Silas and not telling me."

She smiled.

"I don't see you that way, Brianne, and I'm around you way more than Emily, and I've never heard any guy say anything remotely close to that about you."

She thought for a moment about why it hurt so much, and she shared her thoughts with him. "I guess it's that I'm just being me, you know? It's one thing if you do something to hurt someone and they get mad at you, or if someone tells a blatant lie, but Emily and Justine and Brooke don't like me for who I am."

"I wouldn't include Brooke in that."

"She was there!"

"But you know Brooke. She's quiet and never says anything bad about anyone. She probably didn't know what to say, just like you didn't."

Brianne supposed he was right. Brooke had often said she wished she could be friends with guys like she was, not accused her of having five different boyfriends.

"And if *you* had been there?" she asked him. "What would you have said?"

He smiled. "I would have said, 'She only has one boyfriend, and it's me.'"

She laughed. "I'm serious."

"I would have said, 'You know Brianne better than that, Emily. She's not an Ashlee. She's one of your best friends, and you're lucky to have her, just like me.'"

"Really? You're not saying that to spare my feelings?"

"I'm saying it because it's the truth. And if anyone knows the way you are around guys, it's me, Brianne."

She gave him a hug. "Thanks for making me talk about it. I feel better."

"Don't let girl-drama spoil your week. You've been waiting all summer for this."

"I know."

Hearing footsteps on the path, Brianne turned and saw Josh and Anna. They saw them also and came to meet them. She had seen them off and on today, but this was the first time when she wasn't with a bunch of other people.

"Hey, guys. What are you doing down here?" Anna asked. "Aren't you supposed to be getting ready for campfire?"

She asked in a curious way, not an accusing one, but Austin gave her their legitimate excuse. "Brianne had something she needed to talk about."

"Everything all right?" Anna asked.

"Yes," she said, smiling at Austin and then looking back at Anna. "A good talk with your best friend always helps."

Anna smiled and glanced at Josh. "Yes, I know what that's like."

They all turned to walk toward the cabin area, and she and Austin talked to their new youth leaders along the way. She knew Josh and Anna had come along this week to get to know them, and Brianne was enjoying getting to know them too. They had been friends since they were thirteen, had been dating for a little over a year, and they were getting married next month.

Austin left them to go change when they reached the trail to the guys' cabins, and Anna and Josh kept walking with her. Once it was just her and them, Anna asked if she was really all right or if she needed to talk more.

Brianne wanted to talk to Anna too, like she had talked to Megan last night before this latest development. She didn't know if she needed to talk about how Justine and Emily were acting toward her as much as talking about herself and the choices she was making to have guys as friends. She supposed Anna could relate because she had been friends with Josh for ten years before she ever dated him.

"I could talk to your counselor about missing campfire tonight if you want to talk instead," Anna said, "or I could meet you sometime tomorrow. Whatever you need. That's what I'm here for."

Brianne had always enjoyed campfire, and she didn't want to miss that. "Tomorrow would be fine," she said. "How about after lunch?"

"That's good for me."

"Thanks, Anna," she said, giving her a hug and saying good-bye for now.

On the short walk to the cabin, Brianne thought about how quiet Josh had been for the last ten minutes. She knew Brooke was the same way, and she decided to believe Brooke didn't feel like Emily did, even if she hadn't said so. Besides Austin, Brianne considered

Brooke to be her best friend at home, and she didn't want that to change.

When she entered the cabin, several of the girls wondered where she had been, including Sarah who sounded more concerned for her than the others.

"We were getting worried."

"Sorry," she said. "I was talking to Austin."

Sarah smiled like that was a perfectly acceptable excuse, but Justine had another opinion. She voiced it, but Sarah defended her.

"Spending time with Austin doesn't make him her boyfriend," was all she said, but it was enough for Brianne. If Austin and Sarah believed in her, that was enough.

"What's all this talk about boyfriends?" Kit Kat interrupted. "You're only thirteen, girls. There's plenty of time for that later."

"We know," Sarah said confidently. "We're waiting until we're sixteen at least, right Brianne?"

"Yep," she said. "That's what we decided."

"Good for you," Kit Kat said. "And wait for the right guy too, even if you don't meet him until you're eighteen or twenty-five."

Walking up to the Fireside area with all of her cabin mates, Brianne didn't try to walk with any particular person, but when Brooke fell in step beside her, she made an effort to talk to her specifically.

"How did your afternoon go?" Brianne asked. "Did you make a bracelet?"

"Yes, but it's not finished," she said. "I have to go back tomorrow."

Brianne almost said she would go with her, but she remembered she was meeting Anna after lunch and had promised Austin a canoe ride at two o'clock. She decided to wait and see what tomorrow held before she committed herself to anything else.

But she did say something she truly meant. "It's really great having you here this week. I'm glad you decided to come."

"Me too," Brooke said. "Thanks for talking me into it."

Chapter Five

"How long have you and Austin been friends?" Anna asked.

Brianne thought back to when she had moved to Clatskanie in the fifth grade. "When we first moved three years ago I got to know him, but more as a boy who was the same age as me. But in sixth grade he liked Sarah, so he hung around us more, and I think the three of us became friends. Then when Sarah moved last year, it was just me and Austin, and we continued to be friends, but in a different way."

"What way?"

"I don't know," Brianne laughed. "It surprised me, and it's hard to describe. Like me and Sarah were friends, but different because he's a boy, not a girl. We spent time together in different ways than me and Sarah had, but I could talk to him and have fun with him like I'd always been able to with Sarah."

Brianne had already told Anna what had upset her yesterday, and Anna had agreed with Austin about not letting it get to her, but Anna was interested in knowing about the different relationships she had with guys and girls, and Brianne felt comfortable talking about it. She was being honest, and none of her relationships were something to be ashamed of.

"Do you want to know how Austin's dad described your relationship when I first heard about it?"

"Sure," Brianne replied.

"He said, 'If there's one friendship I'm glad Austin has right now, it's his friendship with Brianne. She's had the greatest positive influence on him, and I know that's not changing.'"

"He's had a positive influence on me too," she said. "I think we're good for each other."

"I would agree," Anna said with a smile. "From what I've seen this week, I can see you have a healthy, balanced friendship."

"If you didn't know better, would you think Austin was my boyfriend by the way I act around him?"

"No. And I wouldn't think you were trying to get him to be your boyfriend either. I think your behavior with him and your other guy-friends is totally appropriate, and if that ever changes, I'll talk to you about it, okay?"

"Okay," she said. "I have no idea what I'm doing with this growing-up stuff."

"It doesn't show," Anna said. "I'm not just saying that. I'm more than capable of telling you what I really think. Just ask Josh."

Brianne laughed. "He's quiet."

"Yes, he is. Always has been. And it's one of the things I like best about him."

"When did you know you wanted him as more than a friend?"

Anna smiled. "When he told me he wanted that."

"Really, that's it?"

"Pretty much. I knew for him to say that, he had to be serious, and I knew I wanted it too."

"What am I going to do if I end up with more than one of my guy-friends feeling that way when we're all sixteen?"

"Pray about it and follow your heart. And you don't have to wait until then to start praying. I had been praying for a long time I would know when the right guy for me came along, and when Josh told me he thought it was him, I only had about two seconds to decide before he kissed me, but I knew he was."

Anna told her more about what her friendship with Josh had been like when they were thirteen and all the way through their high school and college years. Brianne thought it sounded a lot like her relationship with Austin, only Anna hadn't ever had a girl who was her best friend too, like the way Brianne felt about Sarah and Brooke. Anna's girlfriends were just girlfriends, but Josh was her best friend.

That made her feel better about having Austin as one of her best friends, along with Joel. Anna said no one else could or should decide who her best friends should be, and that being honest with herself about what she wanted would bring her peace, and Brianne knew that was true. Before yesterday when Emily had said that, she had been feeling very much at peace about her relationships with Austin and Joel. It was a loss of peace based on someone else's *opinion*, not facts, that left her feeling alone and confused.

She had been talking with Anna by the lake near the boat dock so they could talk until Austin showed up for their canoe ride. She wasn't sure if he would remember because he hadn't mentioned it when she had seen him earlier today, but he did.

Brianne smiled when he arrived, and Anna did too. The three of them talked for a few minutes before Anna left them alone, and the first ten minutes of the canoe ride she spent telling Austin some of the things Anna had said that agreed with what he told her last night.

"How was your morning?" he asked. "Is Justine still driving you nuts?"

"No. She hasn't said much today. This morning was mostly about what we're actually doing camp-wise."

"What did you think of that Bible study?"

"It was good," she said. "I liked how it compared the Israelites living in the desert and the Promised Land to the choice we have about doing the same thing now. We can either wander around but never get anywhere, or we can have the faith to go to the Promised Land God has for us and live the blessings."

"Do you feel like you're doing that?"

"Yes."

"Me too," he said.

After their canoe ride they went to get a snack and sat on a bench, drinking their sodas and eating licorice, waiting for their friends to come by the well-traveled area, but they didn't see anyone except Marissa and Kayla, who had gone horseback riding and were on their way to take showers again today.

Austin said he wanted to see Joel's lookout tower, so she took him there, and he was very impressed—to the point of thinking he could never compete with Joel for her heart. She laughed and kept her thoughts to herself. When she had been here with Joel on Sunday night, she hadn't been able to imagine him kissing her like she had last month on their walk by the lake, but she could imagine it with Austin for some reason. Not now, but someday. Like when they were both sixteen and working here at camp together.

On their way back to the main area of camp, Brianne decided she'd better check the craft shop to see if Brooke was there finishing her bracelet, and she was, but she was there by herself. Emily and Justine had gone swimming instead. Brianne felt bad Brooke was all alone, but Brooke didn't seem to mind. Some girls from another cabin were there, and she had been talking to them.

Brianne and Austin decided they would make bracelets too. They were friendship bracelets, and they each chose their own colors. Brianne took an assortment of different shades of blue, and Austin chose pink, purple, and white. Brianne had made them before, but Austin hadn't, so she taught him. Brooke said she was making hers for her sister, and Brianne had in mind to give hers to either Sarah or Austin or Joel, but she didn't decide for sure until Austin gave his to her when he was finished.

Brooke had been doing a more complicated one than they were, but she had finished fifteen minutes ago and left to go write a letter to her sister and put the bracelet in with it.

"Thank you," she said after Austin had tied the ends together around her wrist. She was still working on hers but was almost finished.

"It's not quite a tree fort," he said. "But you can take this wherever you go."

She smiled. "You know what I like best about you, Austin?"

"What?"

"You're not embarrassed about having a best friend who's a girl."

"Why would I be embarrassed?"

"I don't know, but you're not. If one of your friends was always accusing you of being my boyfriend, you'd probably say, 'Call it whatever you want. I just like being with her.'"

"That's the truth," he said.

"I know, and you're not embarrassed by it. That's the impression I got about Anna and Josh today too. Neither of them were embarrassed about their friendship with each other. Neither of them felt like they had to defend it, they just let it be."

"Are you embarrassed about us?" he asked.

"No, but sometimes others make me feel like I should be."

Neither of them said anything else until she finished the bracelet and turned to put it on his wrist.

"You don't have to give me yours just because I gave you mine," he said.

"I know, but I want to. And I want it to be a reminder of what we just talked about. We're friends, and that's okay. No matter what anyone else says. No one can tell us what our friendship should be like except for you and me and Jesus."

Once they were walking back, Austin said something else. "You know what I like best about you, Brianne?"

"What?"

"You let each of your friendships be unique. I don't feel like I need to have the same kind of friendship with you as Sarah has with you, or Joel does. I can be your friend in the way I want to be, and you accept that."

Brianne knew that was true, but it wasn't something she thought about or worked at. She supposed she knew each of her friends were different, and she didn't expect them to be the same. After dinner while they had free time, she asked Brooke if she wanted to go for a walk with her to see Joel's lookout tower. She had promised her they would go sometime, and she also wanted to talk to her about what Emily had said. The more she thought about it, the more she knew Brooke hadn't said anything bad behind her back. Brooke didn't do that with anyone.

Brianne told her about overhearing Justine and Emily yesterday, not saying anything about her not defending her. But she did ask if she felt that way too—like she was a big flirt.

"No," Brooke said. "I couldn't believe Emily said that. That is so not true. I didn't know what to say."

"Don't tell her I know. I'm not going to hold it against her, but I want to make sure I'm not acting like that. And I trust your judgment."

"You're not, Brianne. I think she's jealous of you, Justine too. You're so natural around guys. It's disgusting!" Brooke admitted, but in a funny way.

"I'm just being myself."

"I know. I don't know how you do that."

"You do it too."

"Nuh-uh. I don't say anything most of the time."

"I know, but that's you. You're quiet around a lot of people, not just guys."

"Do you think that's bad?"

"No, that's you. You're like Josh. Have you noticed how quiet he is?"

"I haven't really thought about it."

"He is, but it's not like he isn't there. Anna does most of the talking, but I see them both when they're together."

They had reached the lookout tower, and they climbed up the steps. Brooke said what everyone did when they got to the top and saw the view. "Wow. Joel made all of this?"

"Yep, pretty amazing, huh?"

"No kidding."

They went upstairs and sat on the benches like she and Joel had done on Sunday night. Brianne thought of something before Brooke said it.

"Joel is quiet too, like Josh. I didn't notice that at first because he's talkative with you, but he's not so much with anyone else."

"I know. I noticed that when me and Sarah and Austin were here last month. When it's just him and me, we talk a lot, but not when others are with us."

"Do you think a quiet person like me will be talkative with the right person?"

"Yes. I think if we asked Anna if Josh is talkative when it's just the two of them, she would say yes. I can't imagine them being best friends, let alone engaged, if Josh never talks to her."

Brianne told her what Austin had said about her treating each of her friends uniquely, and she asked Brooke if she agreed with that.

"Yes. I always feel like I can be me with you."

"And that's who I like," she said. "You. Just for who you are."

"I like you for who you are too, Brianne. I think you're the nicest person I've ever met, and you're the best friend I've ever had."

"And you're one of my best friends too. I'm sorry I abandoned you yesterday. I was hurt by what Emily said, and I couldn't be around her."

"I felt that way too. That's why I didn't go swimming with them today. I knew I would rather be by myself than listen to them talk about how many "dates" you had lined up this afternoon."

Brianne didn't ask Brooke what else they said about her. She didn't want to know, and she didn't want to put Brooke in a position of having to rat on them either. She changed the subject and talked about her time in Washington and her time here with Austin and Sarah last month, since she hadn't had a chance to tell Brooke about any of that yet. They had to head back for the meeting, but Brianne knew she could sit up there talking to Brooke for another hour. She hadn't seen her much this summer, and she had missed her.

Over the next couple of days, Brianne had time with all of her friends on an equal level. She hung around with whomever wanted to do the same things she did during any free time they had. During organized meetings, their whole group usually sat near each other along with Josh and Anna. They had their own cabin counselors here, but she felt like Anna was her counselor too, and she had several more chances to talk with her. More so in general than talking about her friendship with Austin.

They talked about the time Anna had spent here as a staff member, and Brianne knew she wanted to do the same thing. Anna said she would fit in well here. It could be a lot of hard work, but definitely worth the friendships she had made and the growth in her relationship with God.

Brianne thought the speaker this week had good things to say, but what she had heard a month ago from the youth pastor during Family Camp was what she had most needed to hear at this point in her faith journey. She told Anna about it on Thursday afternoon, and Anna's response wasn't surprising.

"I never let go, Brianne, and I have ended up with far more by hanging on to God and His love for me than if I had reached for a hundred other things."

Chapter Six

After talking with Anna, Brianne headed back to the cabin and found Sarah there by herself. Other than a few brief moments here and there, she hadn't had any time alone with her, and she wondered where Briana was.

"She wasn't feeling well and went to see the nurse."

"Do you want to go to the store with me?" she asked. "Or are you waiting for her to come back?"

"She's been gone for awhile. I think she must be lying down there. I was going to go check on her, but we can go to the store first."

"Okay," Brianne said, getting some money out of her bag. "I want to get one of those "He loves me" shirts like you got. Do they have any color besides blue?"

"Yes," Sarah smiled. "They have pink."

"Yea!" she said. "I hope they aren't all gone. I meant to get one earlier in the week, but I kept forgetting."

They left the cabin and walked toward the camp store. On the way there Sarah voiced what she had been thinking. "This is the first time we've done something this week, just you and me."

"I know," she said, linking arms with her. "I don't want to think about having to say good-bye to you until who-knows-when."

"I'm sorry we haven't had more time together," she said. "But I didn't want to abandon Briana."

"It's fine," she said. "I really like her, and I'm glad you've made a good friend at school besides Ryan. How is he, by the way? Have you had much time with him this week?"

"Not just him and me, but I think he's having a good time. I'm glad he's in Austin's cabin. They seem to be getting along well, and I think Ryan needs good guy-friends like that. He's made some friends this year besides me, but they're not like Austin."

"Austin and Joel are becoming good friends too."

"Austin has really changed since last summer, Brianne. I think you're a good influence on him."

"How has he changed?" she asked. "I think it's hard for me to see because I see him all the time."

"He's more social and less bothered by what other people think. I saw him earlier and he was talking with Ashlee and Caitlin. I know he can't stand Ashlee, but he wasn't acting like it. He was being nice to them and seemed genuinely interested in how their week was going."

Brianne got an uneasy feeling at the thought of Austin talking to Caitlin. She still wondered if Caitlin liked him and how Austin would react if she ever let him know that.

"You can stop thinking that right now," Sarah said. "He was just talking to them when we were all getting something at the Snack Shack."

Brianne smiled. "I wasn't thinking anything."

"Yeah, right," Sarah said. "You don't have anything to worry about there. Trust me."

"How do you know?"

Sarah smiled. "Let's just say Austin and I had a good talk about you."

"You did? What did he say?"

"I can't tell you, but it's good. I promise."

"Sarah! Tell me!"

"Nope. He swore me to secrecy."

"You're my best friend. Best friends don't keep secrets."

"They do if it's a good secret and in their friend's best interest."

They had reached the camp store, and their conversation about that ceased. It was too small of an area to talk about anything personal. Everyone would hear them. Brianne looked for a shirt in her size and found one. They looked around a little more, and she picked up a small stuffed kitty for Beth. It was gray with black stripes. She also got a notepad set for her mom.

After they left the store, they went to check on Briana, and the nurse said she was lying down on one of the beds, so they didn't bother her. She had woken up with a sore throat this morning. Brianne felt bad Briana was sick, but she welcomed the remaining free time and dinner with Sarah all to herself.

Josh and Anna took their whole group on a hike to Hidden Falls instead of them going to game time after the evening meeting. Ashlee and Caitlin went too, and it was the first time Brianne had seen them much this week. She hadn't been deliberately avoiding them, but Ashlee and Caitlin had mostly hung around with each other and the girls in their own cabin.

Josh and Anna wanted everyone to share about how their week was going and anything significant they were learning about God. Brianne was surprised by how many shared serious things, even Tim and Jason, who weren't always too talkative at youth group or on Sundays. Caitlin shared something very exciting.

"I haven't really heard much about God until this week. I think I've always believed He exists, but I didn't think I could know Him. But this week everyone is telling me I can, and I think that's really cool. My counselor has been talking to me about it a lot, and I want to try and do that as much as I can."

Brianne glanced at Austin sitting on a large boulder across from her in the circle they had made. He was already looking at her, and he smiled and winked. She smiled back, remembering what they had said earlier this summer about their prayers for Ashlee affecting Ashlee's friends too.

Ashlee said something that sounded promising also. She knew God was trying to remind her He was the most important thing in her life, and she knew she wasn't always treating Him like He was. She didn't really share any specific ways she was planning to change that, but Brianne felt hopeful she would be taking her relationship with Him more seriously and allowing Him to guide her. If Caitlin took God seriously after this week, she could see her having a positive influence on Ashlee to do the same.

When it was her turn to share, she talked about not letting go of God's love and the good things He had planned for her, and then Justine shared something that totally blew her away. They hadn't spent much time together this week. Justine had been hanging around with Emily, but Justine said she was glad she had invited her and had been reminded several times that God loved her and she didn't need to be anyone but herself.

"I see Brianne living that way all the time, but I have a hard time believing God loves me the same as her. It will be hard when I go home on Sunday and have to try and live that way without her to remind me."

Her voice got shaky at the end, and Brianne put her arms around her. It was a strange moment where Brianne wasn't sure if she had been treating Justine the way she should and yet not knowing what she could have done differently. It wasn't that she had deliberately ignored her but had been content to let her hang out with Emily if that's what she wanted to do. But apparently Justine had been watching and listening to her more than she thought.

On the walk back she was beside Austin most of the time, and neither of them said anything about anyone else, but she wondered if they were both thinking the same thing. Several of the guys had said something about Austin being a good friend to them and a good example of the way they knew their own lives should be, and Justine, Marissa, Brooke, and Sarah had mentioned her. Brianne didn't feel like she or Austin were trying to be leaders, and yet that's the way others saw them.

They arrived back at the main camp area as the free time after the game was coming to an end. They had ten minutes before they needed to be at campfire, and Austin had a request before they separated to go change into warmer clothes.

"Will you sit by me there?"

"Sure," she said.

"Okay, see you."

Walking back to the cabin and changing into jeans and putting a hoodie over her "He loves me" shirt she had been wearing this evening, Brianne felt lost in her thoughts. Everyone around her was talking about the night-game they would be playing later, and she knew it would be fun, but she had a strange feeling—like God was trying to tell her something, but she wasn't sure what it was.

When they arrived at the campfire area, she looked for Austin but didn't think he was here yet. She was about to sit with the other girls and let him come find her but heard him coming up behind them along with Joel, Silas, and Ryan. She waited to see where they were going to sit, but when he spotted her, he came over to where she was standing and suggested what she had been thinking.

"You can sit by Sarah there, and I'll sit by you."

She did as he said, and the guys sat on Austin's other side. Sarah and some of the other girls said 'hi' to them but once they were talking to each other, Brianne didn't join in on their conversation and turned her attention to Austin instead.

"Are you thinking what I'm thinking?" she whispered.

He smiled at her. "That depends on what you're thinking."

"I feel weird, like God is trying to tell me something, but I don't know what it is."

"If it's the same thing He's telling me, then I do."

"What?"

"It's working."

Splash, the music leader, began leading them in a song, and they stood up with the others, but Brianne kept her focus on Austin.

"What's working?"

"I'll tell you later," he said over the sound of the guitar and the singing voices.

Brianne tried to figure out what Austin meant, and she kind of had an idea, but it wasn't until she had a chance to talk to Austin during the night-game she put it all together. And it meant enough to Austin that he didn't even care about participating in the game, something she knew he had been looking forward to all week.

Chapter Seven

When campfire time ended, Splash gave them instructions to head to the meeting room for details about the game they would be playing. On the way, she walked with Austin and their other friends, but after listening to the game leaders, Austin held her back as everyone else set out to accomplish the mission.

"Would it be all right if we didn't play?" he said. "I'd rather stay here with you and talk."

"You would?"

"I'm not really in the mood for a game."

"Okay," she said.

Austin led her onto the deck off the dining hall where they had been told they could hang out if they didn't want to play. There were about twenty girls there, but besides one guy who had hurt his foot this week and was hobbling around on crutches, Austin was the only guy in the whole camp who was choosing not to participate in the adventurous after-dark game.

They found a place where they could be semi-alone, and Austin didn't waste any time in asking her something. "Have you figured it out yet?"

"Sort of," she said, sharing her thoughts with him. "I know we've been praying for our friends and they're all here plus some of their friends, and God is working in their hearts too. Do you think that's why?"

"Yes," he said, "and it's more than that."

"What?"

"I've prayed for other people before but didn't see much happening, you know?"

"Yeah."

"But ever since last summer, I haven't just been praying for everyone else, but I've been living the truth myself. We both have, and I think that's making the difference."

She could see what he meant. "And He's doing even more than we've asked for?"

"Exactly."

Brianne mirrored his smile. Austin reminded her of his dad in that moment. Pastor Doug was always enthusiastic about seeing kids coming to Jesus in a real way.

"I guess when we don't let go, we help others to hang on too."

"Yes, or grab on if they've been living apart from God."

"I think Sarah was that person for me," she said, remembering after Sarah moved she realized how close to God she was.

"Me too. And you. She got me part way there, but you took over after she left."

"And now she's doing the same thing for Briana and Ryan," she said, recalling both of them had shared some progress in their faith during the time they'd had earlier.

"So, what do we do now?" she asked.

"The same thing, I guess. I realized what was going on when everyone was sharing, because I felt like I wasn't getting a whole lot out of this week—some, but not nearly as much as I got last year and when we were here last month. And when everyone else started sharing, I realized I was already at the places they're just now reaching or hoping to reach. But I know I have further to go, so I'll keep going and hope they follow."

She shared with him what Megan had said on Sunday night about her being a lot different than she had been last summer, and she asked Austin if he agreed with that.

"Yes. Sarah is too."

"And Joel," she added. "But I think that might be because of you."

"Me?"

"He's more social than I've ever seen him. I think you made a new best friend this week."

Austin laughed in a way she knew there was a story behind.

"What's that for?"

"Oh, nothing."

"Austin?"

"We had a good talk about you."

"About me? You talked to Sarah about me too. What are you saying?"

"Did she tell you?"

"No."

He smiled.

"Austin! What!"

"It's nothing you don't already know."

"So tell me!"

"I asked Sarah to hold me to my promise to wait for you, and I—"

"You never promised me that," she interrupted. "I don't expect you to."

He smiled. "I promised myself, not you. And I told Joel I would accept it if you choose him over me someday and I won't hold it against him. I hope the four of us are still friends, no matter what happens between you and me."

"What did he say?"

"You'll have to ask Joel."

"I can't believe you would rather sit here and talk with me than play the game. You've been looking forward to this all week."

He shrugged. "It's just a game."

"If you want to go play now, we can. I'm sure there's plenty of time left. You're the only boy in camp who's not out there, except for that poor guy."

"Two guys and twenty girls? I'd say that's pretty good odds for me. What do you want to bet I could get at least one of them to kiss me?" he said, sitting forward on the bench like he was about to go ask.

She laughed. "Sit down. Kissing is against the rules here, Austin Lockhart."

"Oh, yeah. Well, maybe I can get a date."

She pulled him back toward her. "You just told me about the promise you made, remember?"

He leaned back against the bench and turned to look at her. "I remember."

"Do you want to play?" she asked.

He smiled. "I have a better idea."

"What?"

"Come on," he said, rising from the bench and heading toward the stairs.

She followed him, and once they were away from the light of the deck area, it was pitch black. The lights that were normally on had been turned off for the game. He led them down a trail behind the meeting room and up toward the lake instead of taking the main road that was guarded and would only get them a ticket to "jail".

"Slow down!" she whispered. "I can't see a thing out here."

He reached out and took her hand, and he did slow down a little, but she mostly had to trust he wasn't going to make her smack right into a tree.

"Let's go through here," he said, turning to lead them up a short embankment she knew led to the lake. He kept holding her hand, and she followed behind him through the heavy brush, but within a few seconds they were in the clearing.

He stopped to wait and listen for any staff members who might be guarding this area, but they didn't hear anything except in the distance.

"Come on," he whispered, crossing the road in front of them.

"Where are we going?" she asked.

"Just over here," he said, stepping onto the grassy area overlooking the lake. She could tell where they were now. Her eyes had adjusted, and she recognized the familiar slope and wide-open area.

They walked about halfway down, and it was obvious there wasn't anyone around. They could hear voices and see flashes of light coming from the surrounding wooded areas, but the lake area wasn't a major thoroughfare—which made sense because otherwise people might accidentally fall into the water.

"Here, this will do," Austin said, letting go of her hand and sitting down on the grass.

She sat beside him as he lay on his back, and she realized what he had in mind. Lying beside him, she lifted her eyes to the black sky and saw the brilliant canopy of bright stars above them. It was a spectacular sight she had seen many times here, but she was awestruck every time. And with no camp-lights on right now, it was more beautiful than ever.

"I've wanted to do this all week," he said. "But they always send us to bed right after campfire, and last night our cabin slept outside, but it was cloudy."

Lying there quietly for several minutes, they looked at the stars and listened to the crickets chirping and frogs croaking. She also heard fish jumping in the lake. This was something she had done with Joel, with her cabin mates when they had slept outside, and with Sarah and Austin last month. But this was the first time she had with just Austin, and with their conversation still on her mind and all the things their friends had said earlier, Brianne had a unique feeling and expressed her thoughts.

"You're amazing, Jesus," she said. "I can't believe You show us this every night, even when we don't bother to look."

Other than speaking those few words, they both remained silent until they heard the bell ringing that signaled the end of the game. On the way back, Austin asked if she would spend part of the afternoon with him and Joel tomorrow along with Sarah, saying he and Joel had been talking on the way to Hidden Falls about the four of them having some time together.

"Briana is invited too because I know Sarah won't want to go without her."

"Okay," Brianne said. "And I'll invite Brooke."

The following afternoon Joel took them to a spot along the creek he had discovered earlier this summer. A large tree had fallen across the water this winter, creating a natural dam in a partially sunny area, and the pool of water backed up behind it was wide and deep enough for cooling off and having a good water fight.

They spent two hours together, and by the time they separated to go take showers before dinner, Brianne was almost certain of something she had been suspecting for the last couple of days: Briana liked Joel. They were both more on the quiet side, but they talked to each other quite a bit, and Brianne was reminded of when she and Brooke had talked about not being shy with the right person.

Later when she mentioned something to Sarah about it, Sarah confirmed Briana did have a major crush on him.

"Does that bother you?" Sarah asked.

"No," she said. "I want a nice girl for Joel, and Briana fits that category."

Sarah didn't say anything else, but Brianne realized after she spoke why Sarah had asked that. If Briana had been that way with Austin instead of Joel, it might have bothered her.

That night Brianne was looking at the same spectacular display of stars as she and Austin had last night, only with her cabin mates and their counselor. They had decided to sleep outside, and being able to lie there for more than a few minutes, Brianne saw a lot of shooting stars too.

The canopy of stars reminded her of God's promise to Abraham she had read about earlier this year, and that made her think of Isaac and Rebekah and their love story. After most of her friends had fallen asleep, she was still lying there awake, and she prayed with her eyes open, fixed on the beautiful night sky.

"Whomever I marry, Jesus, I want to be his beautiful virgin bride, and I want us to love each other forever."

In the morning Brianne felt sad about it being the last day, more so than she had anticipated. She had no idea when she was going to be seeing Joel or Sarah after this, and she wasn't only going to miss them individually but also being here with all of her best friends at the same time.

After saying good-bye to Joel, she got into the van and sat beside Sarah. Austin had decided to ride in the other van with the guys this time, and since everyone was tired, the ride to Portland was mostly quiet. She thought Austin might switch vans after they dropped Sarah, Briana, and Ryan off in Portland, but he didn't, and she sat with Justine and talked to her more than she had all week.

By that afternoon it was just the two of them back at her house, and they told her mom and dad about their week. Justine didn't say anything about her having five different boyfriends or talk about Austin and Joel. Justine's mom was coming down from Seattle tomorrow to pick her up, and Brianne had been dreading these remaining hours they would have together, but it wasn't so bad.

Even when they went to her room so she could unpack and there was a letter waiting on her desk from Alex, Justine didn't go overboard in her comments. Brianne read the letter and then let Justine read it too. The only thing she commented on was he had signed it, 'Love, Alex.' But otherwise she left her alone.

Brianne was surprised he had written to her, and she wondered if she should write him back. She decided to the following day after Justine left with her mom, and she told him about her week at camp—leaving out the difficult moments between herself and Justine and any details about her relationship with Joel or Austin, other than to say it had been great to be at camp with her friends.

She mailed the letter on Monday and got another letter back from him on Friday. School didn't start until the following Tuesday, so she'd had an uneventful week, and other than a letter from Sarah on Wednesday, this was the only mail she had gotten.

Dear Brianne,

Thanks for writing me back. It was good to hear from you and all about your week at camp. I'm glad you had a good time. It sounds like a cool place. We go to a camp up here every summer too, and this year was by far the best. I can't wait to go again next year. Maybe you could come with us. I'm sure Katie would love to have you there, and I would too.

Yes, school starts next week. I'm playing football again this year, and we're already having practices. Last year I was the quarterback on JV, but this year I'm on Varsity, and I'm sort of nervous about it. More people than just parents come to watch, and our team has done well in our league the last few years, so the pressure's on. If you could pray for me, I'd appreciate it.

How can I pray for you? That's neat you have new youth leaders you like and your youth building is almost finished. Keep me posted on how all of that is going. Is your group going on any retreats or to any concerts this fall? How about your family? Are you going to be coming up to visit your grandparents at Thanksgiving or Christmas? I'll look forward to seeing you whenever you do.

I hope your school year gets off to a good start, and I'd love a letter from you anytime. Send me a school picture of you if you have *enough. Katie has a picture of you from the Fair, but she wouldn't let me have it.*

You're a nice girl, Brianne. I really liked spending time with you that day. And I hope we can do it again sometime.

Love,
Alex

Chapter Eight

On Tuesday morning when Brianne boarded the bus for the first day of her eighth grade year, along with J.T., Silas, and Danielle, she compared her schedule with Silas' and saw they had three classes together: math, English, and science. She already knew she had three classes with Austin because he had called her to compare their schedules the day they got them.

"I think Austin has science then too," she said, pointing to their last class of the day.

"Yeah," Silas confirmed. "He's bummed you only have three classes together."

Brianne was too, especially since one of them was *Concert Band* where they didn't get to sit by each other, but she had prepared herself for the possibility. She normally didn't have all of her classes with one of her best friends.

When Austin got on the bus five minutes later, he sat beside her, and they did have their first class together. The teacher they had for history was new, so they didn't know what to expect. Mr. Edwards seemed nice and didn't make them sit in alphabetical order, so she was able to keep her seat in front of Austin and beside Brooke.

The rest of the day was mostly uneventful, as was the rest of the week. She didn't see Austin or any of her friends outside of school except for at youth group on Thursday night, and that was the highlight of her week. They hadn't had it last week because Austin's family had gone camping, and she had been gone for several weeks before that, so it was good to get back to seeing her church friends and having that regular time as a group.

On the whole her eighth grade year got off to a good start, but she felt a little overwhelmed with all the homework. She didn't think it was more than she'd had last year, but it was hard to get back into the habit.

That Saturday they had their annual barbecue at the park where they welcomed the new sixth and seventh graders into the group, and it was weird for Brianne to have J.T. there, just like having him at camp last month and at youth group on Thursday night, but she tried to be a good big sister about it. He seemed too young and immature to her, but she knew Austin and the other eighth-grade guys had been the same way.

Ashlee and Caitlin were there too. They'd been at church last Sunday and at youth group on Thursday, and as far as she could tell, their week at camp had changed both of them in a few ways. For one thing, they both talked to her as if they'd been friends for years, and they seemed to take the serious stuff seriously. Brianne had kind of a strange feeling whenever she was around them, almost like she couldn't believe they were here, and also wondering how long it would last. With Ashlee having her ups and downs in the past, she hoped she would remain "up" this time, but she knew that could be a difficult thing to do.

Having Anna as a leader was awesome, and Brianne could see her being someone to keep Ashlee more on the right track spiritually and also help Caitlin in her newfound faith. The youth building was almost complete, and that seemed to have everyone's spirits up about this being a good year for them as a group. After dinner Pastor Doug announced they were hoping to be in there by sometime next month, which Brianne already knew, and everyone was very excited about the announcement.

Brianne also knew her dad and Pastor Doug were talking about the possibility of hiring someone else as a full-time youth pastor now that the new building was almost finished. At this point they were thinking if they did hire someone, they would do it next summer, but that wasn't official news yet, so the only person she could talk to about it was Austin.

He seemed fine with the prospect, and she was too, but there was a part of her that wanted things to stay as they were. But for today she didn't think about it and cheered along with everyone else when Pastor Doug announced they would be going on a retreat on the first weekend in October. They were going to the beach. They were also going to a concert in Portland a couple of weeks after that, and Brianne wondered if she might be able to see Sarah then.

She called her that evening to ask about the concert and also to see how her first week of school had gone.

After they had talked for awhile, Brianne decided to tell Sarah about something on her mind.

"Do you remember that guy I told you about up in Washington I spent time with at the Fair?"

"Yes. Alex, right? I met him when we were there."

"Oh yeah, I forgot that."

"So, what about him?"

"He's been writing to me."

"Letters?"

"Yes."

"Since when?"

"I got the first one the same day I came home from camp, and I wrote him back, and he's sent me two more since then. I didn't respond to his second one, but he wrote me again anyway."

"How do you feel about that?"

"I'm not sure. He surprised me. He never told me he would write in the first place. He must have asked Katie for my address."

"When did you get the third one?"

"Yesterday."

"Did you write him back?"

"Not yet. I didn't have time today, and I'm not sure if I should or not. I don't want to be rude, but I don't want to give him the wrong idea either."

"What are his letters like?"

"Mostly about what he's doing, but he's asked me a bunch of questions too. I feel like I should write him back, but—"

"I don't think there's any harm in writing him," she said. "If he tries to make it into something you don't want, you can always tell him that."

"That's what I was thinking, but guys don't write letters like girls do. I feel like the fact he's writing me is enough to let me know he's hoping for something."

"Maybe, but he could turn out to be a good friend."

"Like that's all I need," she laughed. "Another guy-friend to choose between when I'm sixteen."

"You can't worry about that, Brianne," she reminded her. "Have you prayed about it?"

"Sort of. But it seems like a silly thing to pray about."

"Do it anyway, Bree. It won't seem silly three years from now if he ends up being your boyfriend because God told you to start writing to him now."

"Okay, I will."

"Thanks for letting me know about the concert. I'll talk to my mom and dad and let you know."

"Okay."

"Do you want to plan on spending that weekend with me if they say it's okay?"

"Sure."

"Okay. I'll ask. Love you."

"Love you too."

She asked her mom and dad if that would be all right, and they said it was, and then she went to her room to have time with Jesus and maybe write back to Alex if she felt God telling her to do that.

She did, and reading over all of his letters, she decided to respond to his questions. It was different than writing to Sarah or Joel because she didn't know him well, but she felt free to be herself on paper like she had been when she spent time with him at the Fair.

She also wrote a letter to Joel that was much shorter and mostly informative about her week and her youth group's upcoming plans. And then she wrote to Justine too, but she didn't say anything to either of them about writing to Alex. Nor did she tell Austin or any of her other friends here until two weeks later when Brooke came over on Friday afternoon to spend the night at her house, and she showed Brooke the five letters Alex had written to her since seeing him last month.

"How many times have you written him?"

"Four, but one of them I just sent yesterday, so he probably won't get it until tomorrow."

"Why didn't you tell me he wrote you?"

"I didn't think it was that big of a deal, and I didn't know if he would keep writing me, but he did. I've always been the kind of person who will write back if someone writes to me, and the other person is usually the one to stop, but he's not stopping!"

Brooke read through a couple of the letters, including the one she had gotten this week. Brianne wanted her to read that one because it seemed the most obvious about Alex liking her as more than a friend, but she wondered if she was reading too much into his words.

"I think someone has a crush on you," she confirmed. "How do you feel about that?"

"I have no idea," she laughed.

"So, was there any truth to what Justine was saying about the two of you?"

"I didn't think so at the time. Honestly. I'm used to spending time like that with Austin and Joel, so to me it wasn't any different, but maybe to him it was."

"I think you've got that right," Brooke said.

"The weird thing is, after I decided to write him back last week, I told myself if he wrote me again I would wait a week before writing him, but both times I ended up writing him back that same night. It was like I couldn't help it. He's really easy to write to."

"Is that true of everyone you write?"

"No. I tried to write a letter to Austin this summer when I was at my grandparents', and I couldn't do it, and I've had trouble writing to Joel too. And Justine. She's written me twice since camp and I've only written to her once. I owe her one right now, but it doesn't come easy like when I've written to Alex."

"Does she know about this?"

"She knows about the first letter because she was here when I got it, but I haven't told her about the others."

"Have you told Austin?"

"No."

Brooke raised her eyebrows. "You tell him everything."

Brianne knew she had been avoiding it. "I know, and I know I should tell him, but I haven't."

Chapter Nine

Brooke's mom came to pick her up on Saturday at three o'clock. Her family was going to a wedding this evening at their church in Longview, and Brooke needed to go home and get ready. Brianne asked for a ride to the mailbox and said good-bye to Brooke at the end of the driveway.

"Tell me if you get any more letters from Alex," she whispered out the window before her mom pulled the car onto the country road.

Brianne laughed and waved, then turned to the mailbox to see if there was anything for her today. She didn't expect anything from Alex because she had already gotten a letter on Wednesday, but she thought there might be one from Sarah or Joel. She hadn't heard from Joel since writing him last week, and it had been a few days since she'd heard from Sarah.

Taking the bundle of mail from the box, she looked at the top envelope and saw a letter from Sarah. Closing the mailbox and stepping toward the driveway, she flipped to the next envelope and was excited to see Megan had written her back. She had written to her after camp to let her know how things had turned out with Justine and filled her in on the rest of the week because she hadn't had a chance to talk to her before she left. The envelope after that was from Alex.

She waited until she got to the front porch to open any of them, and she enjoyed the ones from Sarah and Megan, but her mind was more on getting to the one from Alex. She couldn't imagine why he would be writing to her again so soon or what he could possibly have to say, but taking the letter out of the envelope, she could see he had written his normal two pages.

Deciding to say a quick prayer before she read it, she asked God to help her to know what to do about this. Had writing to Alex been a mistake? She hadn't thought so at the time, but maybe it hadn't been a good idea. Letting her eyes fall on the first page, she was about to start reading when her mom came out the front door and told her she had a phone call from Austin.

"Hi, Aus. What's up?" she asked, laying the letter from Alex on her lap.

"Is Brooke still there?"

"No, she just left."

"I'm bored. Do you want to do something?"

"Like what?"

"I don't know. Come over and watch a movie?"

Brianne had a few chores she needed to do, and she also had homework this weekend she hadn't done yet. "I'm kind of busy."

"Doing what?"

"Brooke's been here all day and we've been scrapbooking and goofing off. I have homework to do, and my mom asked me to do some laundry and clean the bathroom."

"You can do homework here."

"While we're watching a movie? I don't think so."

"I could help. What do you have?"

"Tons! I can't, Austin. Sorry. Maybe tomorrow."

"But I'm bored now."

"What about Michael or Silas? Maybe they can come over."

"Yeah, I guess."

"What's that mean?"

"It means I'd rather watch a movie with you."

She laughed. "Okay. How about if you come here and help me with my homework until dinner, and then after dinner we can watch a movie."

"Okay. Do you need to ask?"

"Yeah, hold on," she said, getting up from her perch on the steps and going inside. Her dad was using the computer, and she asked him if Austin could come over. He said that was fine, but then her mom came into the room from the kitchen and reminded her about the laundry and the bathroom.

"Yeah, I know. I'll do that now," she said.

"Okay," her mom agreed in her 'I'm trusting you to keep your word on that' voice.

She told Austin it was fine if he came, but he backtracked. "If this isn't a good time, I'll live."

"It's fine," she said. "But you might end up helping me fold laundry."

"Okay by me."

She let him go and took her mail to her room. Laying it on her bed with Alex's letter still unread, she went to the laundry room and put in a load of whites, then went to the hall bathroom to clear off the cluttered countertop, clean the sink and the mirror, and scrub the toilet. Austin arrived as she was finishing up with that, and she told him to play video games while her brothers were outside and she cleaned the tub and shower, but he had a better idea.

"I'll clean the shower and you get started on your homework, but leave the tough stuff for me to help you with."

She laughed. Whenever they did homework together, she usually helped him, but she appreciated his help with the bathroom and handed him the sponge she had used for the sink. "Thanks," she said. "I should have you over on Saturdays more often."

Going back to her room, she was about to grab her backpack and take her books to the dining room when she saw the mail on her bed and decided to read Alex's letter first.

Dear Brianne,

Hi, me again. How are you? It's Wednesday, and I'm in English class. We're having some free-writing time, and I thought I'd write to you again since this is my favorite form of writing right now, and because I can't seem to think about much besides you anyway.

He went on to talk about what his day had been like so far and what he would be doing later: football practice after school, home for a little while, and then youth group. He also told her about some new music he'd gotten, and he wondered if she had the same album. She didn't but it was a CD she had been thinking of getting Austin for his birthday next month.

The ink color changed from black to blue after that, and she knew he must have been interrupted and continued the remainder of the letter later, which he confirmed in the first sentence.

Okay, jump forward a few hours and here I am at home, and it's almost time for me to go to youth group, but I want to finish this letter to you first so I can mail it in the morning. Let's see, where was I? Oh, yeah. The new album I was telling you about. I mentioned it because one of the songs reminds me of what you were saying about not letting go of what we already have to reach for things that won't be any better anyway. If you have it, then you probably know what I'm talking about, but if you don't, these are the words:

He loves me
So what else can I reach for
He holds me
And I'm never letting go

You can have your plans
You can have your dreams
But as for me
I'll just hold on to what He has for me

Wow! If we could get that and never let go? I can't imagine where I would end up. Can you? Letting the God of the Universe plan my life instead of me? Yeah, I'll sign up for that.

Well, I guess that's all I have for today. I hope I'm not assuming anything by writing to you again before you've had a chance to write me back, but I had you on my mind today, and I guess you aren't annoyed by me yet since you've written me back some great letters. I've never written letters to anyone before except for a Compassion kid my family sponsors. He's my age, and he lives in Brazil. But it's hard to talk to someone who lives in another culture sometimes. I thought writing to a girl might be like that too, but so far I find you easy to write to and I hope you feel the same way about me. If you don't, you can stop and I'll take the hint.

Have a great day, Brianne. Until next time...

Love,
Alex

"I know the plans I have for you," declares the Lord. Jeremiah 29:11

Brianne sighed. She had the same feeling of wanting to write back she'd had before, but she knew she didn't have time right now. Taking her journal from her night stand, she stuck all three of the letters inside and went to get started on her homework. But her mind was still on Alex. She took out her math book and did the first couple of problems but then her mind wandered.

She knew she enjoyed writing to Alex, and she didn't see any harm in it, but she didn't want him to read more into her letters than she intended. She was used to having guys as friends, but if he wasn't used to having girls as friends, then he might be taking her letters more seriously than as one friend writing to another.

She was still working on her math when Austin came to join her. Her mind wandered less after that, and Austin helped her with the science questions. The answers were in the book, but sometimes it took some searching to find them, so he helped the process to go faster.

She took a break to put the washed clothes into the dryer and to put a load of towels into the washing machine. Austin asked her something while they were in the laundry room.

"Are you okay?"

"Fine," she replied. "Why do you ask?"

"I don't know. You just seem—kind of distracted, I guess."

"I told you I had work to do," she laughed. "If this isn't more fun than being at home—"

"No, I don't mean that. You're not busy with stuff—you're not here somehow."

She closed the lid of the washing machine and looked at him. Their laundry room was really tiny, and he was blocking the door, so she couldn't walk past him and continue this conversation on their way back to the table. He seemed honestly concerned, and she knew her mind was on Alex. But she wasn't sure what to tell him.

"Best friends, Brianne," he reminded her. He seemed to be doing that more with her lately than she'd had to do with him.

Her brothers had come inside, and they were being loud. She knew this wasn't the best place to talk, and going to the dining room was out of the question. Turning toward the door that led outside, she invited Austin to go for a walk with her. They went around the back of the house and along the side, past where the van and car were parked and onto the driveway.

"I have something to tell you," she said.

"What? You're moving?"

"No," she said. "Not that I know of."

"Okay, let me have it. Anything else I can handle."

She smiled, knowing he was serious but almost not believing him. Austin being important to her, she could understand, but why was she so important to him? She wished she could see what he saw—what he valued so much. Their friendship, or was it more than that? And how was he going to take the news about her writing letters to another guy?

Emily's comment at camp about her having a different boyfriend every week came back to haunt her, and she wondered if Emily was right. She could imagine Austin feeling frustrated with her, and maybe he had every right to be.

Chapter Ten

"You're scaring me, Brianne," Austin said when she didn't answer him. He put his arm around her shoulder. "What's going on?"

She took a deep breath and sighed, wanting to tell him and not wanting to at the same time. But it was too late to pretend she was fine or make up something else.

"Do you remember Justine talking about that guy in Washington I spent some time with at the Fair?"

"Alex?"

"Yes."

"The one Justine insisted was your boyfriend, and you insisted he wasn't?"

"Yes."

"Were you lying about that?"

"No! We only spent a couple of hours together."

"Okay, I believe you," he laughed, dropping his arm from her shoulder. "So what about him?"

"He wrote me a letter."

"When?"

"It was waiting for me when I got home from camp."

"What did he say?"

"Just that he enjoyed getting to know me."

"Did you write him back?"

"Yes, and then he wrote me again, so I wrote him back, and he wrote to me—"

"How many letters?"

"Six, including the one I got today."

Austin stopped walking. "You've written him six letters in a month?"

"No, I've written him four. He's written me six."

"What kind of letters?"

"I don't know, just letters. He tells me about what he's doing, and I do the same back."

"Do you like him?"

"Yeah, I like him. He's nice."

"Is he the same age as us?"

"Yes. He'll be fourteen in January. Our birthdays are like three weeks apart."

"And why is this the first I'm hearing about it?"

"I didn't know how to tell you. It's not a big deal, but—"

"But you can't stop thinking about him?"

"No," she laughed. "It's not like that."

"Not like what?"

"Like, 'I miss him terribly and wish he lived here.'"

"So what are you thinking?"

"I'm wondering why he's writing to me and if he's thinking things about me I'm not thinking about him."

"You could ask."

"I know, and I guess that's what has me distracted today. He told me if I'm annoyed with him writing to me, I could stop writing and he would take the hint, but I do like writing to him."

"But you don't want him to think you like him too much?"

"Yes."

"Then tell him."

Brianne knew it was that simple, and she realized what was bothering her. If Alex stopped writing because she didn't want to be more than friends with him, she could handle that, but if Austin felt hurt or pulled back from their friendship because she was writing letters to Alex, she couldn't handle that.

"Do you mind if I keep writing to him?"

"Why would I?"

"I don't know. Do you?"

"No."

"Are you mad I didn't tell you?"

"No."

She waited for him to be totally honest on that.

"I'm not your boyfriend, Brianne. You can write to whoever you want."

"But if you told me you didn't want me to, I wouldn't."

"Why?"

"Because you're more important to me than Alex."

"Am I?"

"Of course you are."

"It doesn't bother me if you write to him."

She believed him this time, and she felt better.

"Have you told him about our friendship and your decision to not have a boyfriend until you're sixteen?"

"No. I haven't felt like I need to because I see him as a friend, but I probably should, huh?"

"I can't speak for the guy, but if it was me and I'd met a pretty girl from out of town, spent a couple of hours alone with her at the Fair, and then wrote her a letter and she wrote me back, there would only be one reason why I would write her five more in a month."

"And invite her to go to camp with you next summer?"

"Did he?"

She laughed.

Austin shook his head and started walking away from her toward the road like he would rather tell her good-bye now. She went after him and linked her arm with his, but he kept walking.

"You know something, Austin?"

"What?" he replied.

"If I could only have one friend right now, I'd pick you, and you know why?"

"Because I'm your best friend?"

"No, because you're the only friend I couldn't live without."

"How do you know that? You've never had to."

"Yes, I have. This summer I had to a lot, and I didn't like it. One reason why I had such a fun time with Alex that afternoon was because he reminded me of you."

"So why wouldn't you pick him?"

"He reminded me of you, but he wasn't."

"Could he be?"

"What do you mean?"

"If he lived here and I didn't, could you see him being your best friend?"

"I don't know him well enough to say, and it doesn't matter because you are here, and I couldn't be happier about it."

Brianne waited a few days before writing Alex back. She was busy, and she wanted to wait and see if he responded to her most recent letter first. She had said something in it about her family's plans to go to Bellingham for either Thanksgiving or Christmas, and she wondered if he might suggest them seeing each other then, and he did. She got the letter on Wednesday.

> *That's great you're coming up again so soon, I can't wait to see you. Do you think your mom and dad would let you spend part of a day with me? Maybe we could go ice skating and then see a movie or something?*

She wrote him a long letter in response, telling him about her decision to only have guys as friends for now. She knew they could do something together while she was there and have it be a friend-thing, but she didn't feel ready for that at this point because she didn't know him well enough to consider him a close friend she would spend extra time with. She told him so but said that might change if they continued writing to each other over the next few months.

> *We should be at church, and I'll look forward to seeing you face-to-face again. I do think you are a nice guy, and I'm enjoying getting to know you better in this long-distance way. I hope I*

didn't mislead you by not telling you any of this before. I like writing to you and getting your letters, and I hope you don't stop, but if you do, I'll understand. And I hope you don't think I'm trying to create a bunch of drama with you, because I'm not. You'll have to take my word on that, but this is who I am, Alex. This is who I'm choosing to be right now. I think being thirteen is complicated enough without adding dating to it. I do have several guys as friends, and they are each special to me in different ways, and I'd love to consider you to be one of them, but that's all I can offer you right now.

That Saturday was Josh and Anna's wedding, and Brianne absolutely loved it. It was the first wedding she had been to where she knew the bride and groom as more than distant family members or people from church she knew by name and face but not personally. Josh and Anna had only returned to Clatskanie last month and been their new youth leaders for the same amount of time, but she had gotten to know Anna, and she could feel the genuine joy of the occasion.

She didn't get to talk to them much, but she admired their love for each other from a distance, and she had several visions of her own wedding day being similar. Assuming her dad remained the pastor here long enough, she could be getting married on this same front lawn. And she could imagine marrying someone she had been friends with for a long time too.

"Are you watching that again?" Austin said, coming up behind her during the reception.

She kept her eyes on the video display of the slideshow Josh had put together and had running on his tablet for the guests to view as they waited in line for cake. It was pictures of him and Anna growing up, some of them individually but mostly of them together, from the time they were thirteen all the way through their high school and college days.

Now that everyone had gotten their cake, she had come over to watch it again, and she felt no shame in it. "Yes, I am," she said, responding to Austin's light teasing. "And what's your excuse for being over here? More cake?"

"No, I was coming over to ask if you want to meet someone."

"Who?"

"Janie. She's over there talking to my mom and dad, and my dad asked me to come get you."

"Okay," she said, turning away from the table to walk with Austin. Janie had been at church on Sundays for the last month, and Brianne had seen her sitting with Josh and Anna, but she hadn't officially met her.

Pastor Doug introduced them to one another when she and Austin arrived, and Brianne smiled at her and received one in return. Janie seemed friendly but shy about meeting her, and yet she did say something that let Brianne know Pastor Doug had talked about her.

"So, you're the famous Brianne. It's nice to meet you finally."

"It's nice to meet you. What's your baby's name?"

"Michael," she said, rubbing his back as she spoke. He wasn't sleeping, but he had his head on her shoulder. "He's about ready for a nap."

Josh interrupted them, and he took Michael from her. "Anna wants to talk to you before we go," he said to Janie. "She's over by the arbor."

"Okay," Janie said. She excused herself from them and headed toward where the ceremony had taken place.

After she was gone, Josh shared the secret with them. Anna wanted to give Janie her bouquet as a symbol of her strong belief that God was going to bless Janie with a loving husband someday who would take care of her and Michael. Brianne hoped so too, and she was reminded of her admiration for Anna. Brianne knew she wanted to be like her when she was in her twenties, and even now as much as she could.

Anna was so loving and kind to everyone. She was sweet and encouraging but also honest and told people what they needed to hear. She reminded her of Megan, someone she had wanted to live closer to the last couple of years. Being lost in her thoughts, she didn't notice when everyone stepped away until Austin said something and she looked up and realized they were alone.

"You know something Josh told me about Anna that reminds me of you?"

"What?"

"She never gave him the option of not being her best friend."

Brianne smiled. "You never gave me that option either."

They knew Anna and Josh were getting ready to leave, so they walked toward where the crowd was gathering to say good-bye to them.

"I wrote back to Alex this week," she said. "And I made a decision about something."

"What?"

"He asked me to send him a picture of me, and I don't have any of my school pictures left from last year, so I was thinking of sending him one from Ashlee's party, but I hadn't yet. I only have one left, and I wasn't sure I wanted him to be the one to have it."

"Did you send it to him?"

"No," she said. "I'll send him one of my school pictures from this year when we get them."

Austin didn't say anything, but she was telling him this for a reason.

"I want you to have it."

"Have what?"

"The picture. My last one."

"You do?"

"Yes. Do you want it?"

He smiled. "Sure."

"I'm going to send it to you in the mail along with a letter I'm writing."

He seemed more curious now. "You're writing me a letter?"

"Yes. I tried to write you one when we were in Washington, but I couldn't, and I figured out why."

"Why?"

"You'll see when you get the letter."

"You can be a real girl sometimes, you know that?"

She laughed. "That's because I am a girl."

"I know," he said. "Believe me, I know."

Chapter Eleven

That night Brianne had a dream she was getting married. In the dream she looked the same, but she was older. She had graduated from college with a teaching degree and she was going to be starting her new job in another week, but they were getting married first.

The wedding was taking place outside like Josh and Anna's wedding, and everything looked similar, but it was at a different place she didn't recognize. Throughout the dream, whomever she was marrying was always beside her, but she never saw his face until he was about to kiss her at the end of the ceremony. It was Austin, but she woke up before their lips could meet.

No! Don't wake up now! She tried to go back to sleep and let the dream continue, but it didn't work. She laid there with her heart pounding and wishing it had been real. Thinking about how old she had been in the dream, she knew that was a lot of years from now, and she didn't want to wait to grow up. She wanted to be like Anna, and she wanted to be like her now.

Going to church and having Anna and Josh not be there because they were on their honeymoon magnified the way she felt. She had been so happy for them yesterday, but today she felt envious. She wanted to have their life, not be thirteen with ten years of school left to go before she would be where they were now.

That afternoon her discontentment surfaced, even though she wasn't thinking about it. She got mad at J.T. over something minor, and she stomped out of the room, knowing she needed to finish her homework anyway. She tried to blame her anger on what J.T. had done, but her mom wasn't buying it.

"Did something happen at church this morning?" she asked, coming into her room.

"No."

"Are you going to tell me what's wrong, or let yourself be mad about it for the rest of the day?"

"Nothing happened!" she said, feeling annoyed at her mom for not believing her instead of being out there punishing J.T. He was the one who had upset her. She had been folding laundry on the couch, and he came to sit down, knocking one of the stacks onto the floor. He helped her refold some of it, but she felt like her ten minutes of work had been a waste of time.

"If you don't want to tell me, fine. But don't lie and say it's nothing."

"Why don't you believe me?"

"Because this isn't like you. What's wrong?"

The depressed feelings came back to her, and she voiced them.

"I want to be a grown-up," she said. "I'm tired of being thirteen!"

Her mom came to sit on the bed beside her and waited for her to say why she felt that way.

"I wish I was old enough to get married like Anna. I had a dream last night I was getting married, and when I woke up I felt disappointed it wasn't real."

Her mom smiled. "It was a nice wedding yesterday, wasn't it?"

"Yes," she said, leaning into her mom. "I want to have a wedding like that."

"I'm sure you will, sweetie."

"But I want to have it now."

"Anna didn't have it when she was thirteen. She had to wait."

Brianne hadn't thought of that.

"What was it like?" her mom asked.

"What?"

"The wedding in your dream."

"It was a lot like Anna's, only in a different place. I'm not sure where."

"And whom were you marrying?"

Brianne laughed. "I couldn't see his face. I could see everyone there, even myself, but I couldn't see him." She decided not to tell her about that changing before the kiss when Austin's face had been unmistakable. "Did you ever have a dream like that?"

"Yes, I think I did. Probably more than once."

"Did you ever dream about marrying Daddy after you met him but before you knew if you would?"

"I don't remember," she laughed. "That was awhile ago."

"How long?"

"Eighteen years since we started dating." Her mom paused and then added. "We have the video of the wedding. Do you want to watch it?"

Brianne remembered watching it once when she was younger, before she understood what getting married was about. She knew she would see it with different eyes now.

"Sure," she said.

They went to her mom and dad's bedroom, and her mom got the video out of a keepsake box on a shelf in the closet. She put it in, and they sat on the bed to watch it. Her parents had gotten married at her grandparents' church in Washington, and it looked almost the same as it did now. Brianne laughed at some of the clothing and hairstyles, but she thought her mom looked really beautiful.

"I know you feel like you want to get married right now, but you know what you don't want to miss out on?"

"What?"

"Meeting the right guy and falling in love with him. It was hard to wait for it, but that was one of the happiest times of my life. I wouldn't have wanted to miss it just to be married."

"Do you wish you had met Daddy sooner?"

"No, not really. I think it was the right time for both of us. If we had met sooner, it would have been different."

Her dad came into the room then, asking what they were up to. Her mom pointed to the television, and he looked to see what they were watching.

"Oh, no. You're not letting her watch that, are you? I think letting her go to the wedding yesterday was quite enough."

"Come watch with us," her mom said, moving over on the bed to make room for Daddy beside her.

He walked over and sat down, putting his arm around her mom and pulling both of them toward him because she was already in her mom's arms. "Fast forward through this boring pastor stuff," he said. "Let's get to the good part."

Her mom did as he requested, and she let it play again when they were saying their vows to one another and exchanged rings. Brianne was reminded of something she'd thought about yesterday when Josh and Anna had done the same thing, but more so now because her parents had kept those vows to one another for the last sixteen years.

One of her friends at school had told her this week her parents were getting divorced. She had known Allison since fifth grade when she moved here. Allie had been in her class along with Sarah, and the three of them had been friends. She hadn't had any classes with her in sixth and seventh grade and had lost touch with her as a close friend, but this year they had three classes together and had been getting reacquainted.

Allie told her about her parents getting divorced during P.E. when they were running the mile. Brianne always felt bad when she heard that about anyone, but she felt really bad for Allie because it was actually her mom's second marriage. Allison's real dad had left when she was two, and she never saw him. Her mom had remarried when Allie was four, and even though her step dad wasn't her real dad, she thought of him that way because he was the only dad she had ever known. He was good to her, and she loved him, but he had never officially adopted her as his own, so now that they were getting divorced, he wouldn't have any legal right or obligation to see her, and she didn't know if he would make the effort.

He had moved out just before school started, and Allie hadn't seen him since, because he had gone to the coast to find a job there. Brianne was praying he would come to visit her soon.

Brianne couldn't imagine going through that, and she felt fortunate she didn't think she would ever see the day her parents would get divorced. They didn't ever fight, and she knew that had something to do with the way they had met, dated, and fallen in love with each other. It hadn't started on the day of their wedding. It had started long before that. Back to when her mom was making decisions about whom to date and kiss and letting God guide her in that.

She felt more content for the remainder of the day, and she didn't think about the dream much that week, but it came to mind once in awhile. She also kept wondering about Alex, especially when he hadn't responded to her letter by Thursday.

They were going to the beach this weekend for the youth retreat, and she had to be at the church by four and still had some packing to do, but when a letter from Alex finally came on Friday, she took the time to read it after she reached the front porch, honestly not knowing what he would say. This had been the longest she had gone without hearing from him, and she had begun to wonder if she ever would again.

Dear Brianne,

I'm sorry it's taken me a few days to get back to you. You probably think I'm mad about what you said in your last letter, but I'm not. I've just been waiting a few days to see if God has anything else to say to me before I wrote you back. And He has, and I'll share that with you in a minute, but let me back up first.

A couple of weeks ago I was feeling really confused about all of this. When I wrote to you the first time, I had no idea why I was. I have enough trouble understanding and connecting with the girls right here in my own school and church, let alone a girl I've only met a few times and wouldn't be seeing again for several months. But I couldn't stop thinking about you and decided to write so maybe next time when you come for a visit, you would remember me and we could talk and have fun together like we did this time. I wasn't looking to have you as my girlfriend, I was just writing to you because I wanted to.

But then when you wrote me back, it did something to my heart (that probably sounds cheesy, but that's the only way I can describe it), and I had to write you back. I regretted it the next day, and I told myself if you wrote me again, I would wait at least a week before writing you back instead of on the same day I got your letter, but then I ended up writing to you before you wrote back to me. I can't explain why I felt like I had to, I just did, and after that whenever I got one of your letters, I couldn't wait to respond. (Am I sounding really desperate and like the biggest loser you've ever met?) Well, at least hear me out because I think the next part is pretty cool. Not cool of me, but cool of you and God.

Then a couple of weeks ago I started to panic, feeling like I had started something I wasn't ready for, but I didn't want to be a jerk and stop writing to you, and when you wrote and said you were going to be here at Thanksgiving or Christmas, I felt like I had to try and arrange a time to see you. That's what a boyfriend does when his girlfriend from out of town comes to visit, right? But the whole time I was thinking, 'I'm thirteen. What do I know about having a girlfriend? What am I going to do, take her out to dinner on my five-dollar-a-week allowance? I knew I was getting in way over my head, but I wasn't about to let you know that. I had to act like your cool boyfriend even if I'm clueless, right?

Needless to say, my saving moment came when I got your letter. I read the whole thing, feeling totally blown away you had given so much thought to your own dating-life that won't *even start for another three years. I've never met a girl like you, Brianne. And I appreciate you being honest without making me feel like the biggest idiot ever.*

After I read it, I heard God saying to me, 'Writing to Brianne hasn't been a mistake. You need a friend like her, and don't be afraid of it. But don't try and make it into something you're not ready for. You can be yourself with her, and you can be honest, because that's what she's going to be doing with you.'

The next day was Sunday, and I went to church seeing the girls in my youth group differently, and the girls at school on Monday too. More of them are probably like you than I think, and the ones who aren't, I shouldn't be bending over backwards to try and impress anyway. My view of God has also changed. After all that talk about letting God be in control of my life, you probably think I've already done that with you and other girls too, but I haven't. I've been thinking of it more in terms of school and sports and my future plans for college, but not so much for what girls I like and the relationships I have now.

But I need to do that, just like you are, and maybe the only reason God wanted me to write to you and gave me the desire in my heart was so I could learn that from you. But if you don't think I'm too big of an idiot, I'd like to keep hearing from you, and I'll keep writing you back—but just as a friend. And I'm more than happy to have it be that way. Honestly, Brianne. I know I'm not ready for more right now, and it's a freeing feeling to know I don't have to be. I can be thirteen and let the girls I know be thirteen and wait for whatever God has planned for me and them in the future.

Your friend,
Alex C. Eastman

(The "C" is for Christopher or clueless, take your pick!)

Chapter Twelve

"You're in a good mood this weekend."

Brianne looked at Austin and smiled. It was Saturday afternoon, and they were having free time on the second day of their youth retreat at the beach. They had been playing volleyball in the sand for the last hour, and she had been acting really goofy. She wasn't a great volleyball player, and everyone knew it, but she'd been having a lot of fun helping her team lose.

"I am," she said, taking a seat on a large piece of driftwood. "Ask me why."

"Why are you in a good mood?" he asked, sitting down beside her. Some of the others were playing another game, but they had pulled out this time and said they would watch.

"I got a letter from Alex yesterday."

He rolled his eyes. "Oh brother. Sorry I asked."

She laughed. "Ask me what he told me."

"I don't want to know."

"Yes, you do. Ask me."

He sighed. "What did he tell you?"

She decided not to tell him the whole story, just the most important part. "He's glad I only want to be friends right now because that's all he wants too. He knows he's not ready for more, and he's glad I feel the same way."

"That's good news," he said.

"I know, and I have you to thank for telling me to be honest with him."

"I learned that from you."

"But we still need to remind each other. This time it was you reminding me."

"Are you still going to write to him?" he asked.

"Yes. I wrote him back last night, and in the letter he told me he would still write to me if I wrote to him."

"What do you like about writing to him?"

"It's easy, and we're becoming friends through it. I've never done that before. Usually I'm already friends with someone I write to, but with Alex it's the opposite."

"Where's my letter you promised me? I waited all week for it, and it never came."

She smiled. "I'm sorry, I should have told you. I'm sending it to you for your birthday."

"My birthday! That's not for a whole week."

"I know. Are you doing anything?"

"Like having a party?"

"Yeah."

"No. Not with my friends anyway. Just our family."

"That's cool," she said.

"But you're invited if you want to come."

"I am?"

"Yes."

She smiled. "Thanks. What time?"

"I'm not sure yet. I'll let you know."

Brianne had already written the letter she planned to send to Austin, but she read it over later that week, and she didn't feel the need to make any changes. It wasn't a long letter, just an extended note explaining why she wanted him to have her picture.

Dear Austin,

I decided I wanted to give you my last picture because you were a huge part of what happened the night of Ashlee's party, and as more time goes by, I can see how much that experience has changed me. You're my hero, Austin, in so many ways, and I know you are a rare treasure. As my friend now and for whatever you may be to me in the future. My life is different because of you, and I want you to have a reminder someone thinks you're special and needs you in her life.

This summer when I was in Washington I tried to write you a couple of times, but I couldn't, which is odd for me because I can usually write to anyone, especially my closest friends. But since we've been back, I've realized talking to you face to face is the best way, and writing to you felt fake—like that's not the way we talk to each other. I don't babble on about stuff and you just listen, I want your input on what I'm saying, and in a letter I knew wasn't going to be returned, I didn't have that.

I hope you have a great 14th birthday, and I hope I'm around to see more years go by for us together, but if I'm not, you will be in my heart on those days too. Life may take us in different directions, but that doesn't change how much a part of my life you are now and how happy I am to have you for a friend.

Love you,
Brianne

Placing the picture and note into an envelope, she mailed it to him, and that evening at youth group she invited him to do something on Saturday with her family. Her brother Steven was joining a Special Olympics bowling league, and their first practice was this weekend. Her whole family was going to watch and support him, and she thought Austin might like to go, so she asked.

"Where is it?" he asked.

"In Longview. It's at one o'clock, and we'll be back in plenty of time for dinner and your party and everything."

"And everything? It's just dinner and cake and opening presents."

"You never know," she teased him. "It could be a huge surprise party, and this is your parents' way of getting you out of the house."

"Or maybe that's what's really happening at the bowling alley?"

"Yeah, maybe," she said. "You'll have to come and find out."

"I'd come anyway," he said. "Thanks for asking me. That will be fun."

It did turn out to be fun, and Steven was very excited Austin was there. Austin had become like another brother to him, especially over the summer. There was no surprise party planned for Austin at the bowling alley or at his house later, but it was fun to watch him wondering about it throughout the day. He said something about it several times as a joke, but she knew he was thinking she might have been serious, especially when her dad dropped them off at his house at five o'clock.

They had gone out for ice cream on their way home from Longview and then Austin had come to their house to play video games with her and her brothers. Lately she had been joining in more than she usually did, and since she didn't have any homework this weekend except the short amount of math she had already completed last night, she didn't have any reason not to today. Austin wanted to play one of his favorite games four people could play at once, and it was her favorite too.

Entering his house without any darkness or large crowd awaiting them, just Mrs. Lockhart who was in the kitchen finishing up with the dinner preparations, they said a quick hello to her and then went into the family room. Austin had told her earlier he had something to show her, and it was a brand new guitar he'd gotten for his birthday from his parents. He had actually gotten it yesterday when they had taken him to a music store and let him pick out the one he wanted.

"It's beautiful," she said. "Play something for me."

He didn't want to, but she coaxed him into it, and she could tell he had gotten a lot better than the last time she'd heard him practicing one day when she had been over here doing some homework last spring.

"I've kind of been working on a song," he said. He took a paper from his stack of music books and handed it to her. "I'm not singing it for you, but you can read the words and I'll play the chords."

Brianne took the lyrics and read them silently as Austin played the music on his guitar, and she was blown away by what she read.

Face To Face

You are love and life and truth
But sometimes it's hard to see
The different forms You take
In everything You are

What I want, Jesus
Is to see You face to face
Maybe that won't be
Until I enter Heaven
Or maybe I can see You today

I was sitting around yesterday
Wondering what life's about
And You spoke so clearly to me
Like I could hear You shout

What I want, child
Is to see you face to face
Maybe that won't be
Until you get Here
Or maybe I could see you today

That's what life's about
Us standing face to face
That's why I made you
And why I died for you
So come and see Me now

She didn't ask him to sing it for her because she knew he would be too embarrassed, but she thought the words were powerful just reading them. Thinking about how she had seen Jesus face to face lately, she knew there were a lot of little things, but one of the greatest was sitting right in the same room with her, strumming notes on his guitar and reminding her of God's goodness.

"You should sing that for youth group sometime," she said, knowing he would probably say he didn't want to, but wanting to encourage him just the same. "Or maybe you could play and let Danielle sing the words. She would love doing that."

"That's a good idea," he said. "I hadn't thought of that, but I had thought of asking you to sing it."

"Me? I don't think so. Danielle is a much better choice."

"You're a good singer," he said simply, like there was no arguing that point. "But if you would be more comfortable singing with someone else, you could ask her.   Maybe we could do it for the New Building Dedication next Sunday."

She laughed. "Then you're going to have to sing it for us so we know how it goes."

"Will you do it?"

"If Danielle will sing with me," she said, feeling nervous about it but also honored Austin would ask her.

"We can practice tomorrow afternoon," he said. "It's simple. You'll pick it up quick."

"Sing it for me now," she challenged him. "I want to hear it."

His mom saved him for the moment, saying dinner was ready and asking Austin to tell his dad and brother, who were outside. He put the guitar on its stand and rose from the chair.

"Before I leave tonight, I want to hear it, Austin," she called after him. "If you don't, I'm not singing."

Chapter Thirteen

After Austin left the room, Mrs. Lockhart asked what that was about, and Brianne shared their idea to have her and Danielle sing the song next Sunday when they had a special service planned in the new building. It had passed the final inspection this week, and the whole church was excited about putting it to good use, even most of those who had been unsupportive of the project along the way.

"That would be perfect," Austin's mom said. "You and Danielle sound good together when you sing, and it's a beautiful song. I overheard Austin singing it one day."

Brianne was surprised to hear her say she and Danielle sounded good singing together. Danielle was the one with the great voice, and she just sang along. Sometimes Danielle would sing harmony and she would stay on the melody, but she didn't have the ability to pick out different notes on her own.

She decided to call Danielle while Austin was outside, and Danielle said she would love to sing it with her. She would be there for their regular band practice tomorrow afternoon. Over the summer they had started practicing on Sundays instead of Saturdays because it usually worked better for everyone's schedules.

Telling Austin as they began to sit down at the table for dinner, she laughed when he said he couldn't believe he had agreed to do such a thing.

"It was your idea," she said.

Pastor Doug came into the room and asked what they were talking about. Austin told him. His dad smiled and winked at her. "I thought he was only going to ask you to sing."

She felt embarrassed. She could never sing by herself and was certain no one would want to listen if she did. "I asked Danielle to sing with me. I'm sure it will sound much better that way."

"It's a nice song," Pastor Doug said. "Don't you think?"

"I like the words, but Austin hasn't sung it for me yet."

Pastor Doug prayed before they ate, and Austin was sitting beside her so they held hands. Austin hung on for an extra moment after the 'amen', and he leaned close to say something to her.

"Thanks for coming tonight. I'm glad you're here."

She was glad too and enjoyed the meal of tacos and Mexican side dishes, Austin's favorite food besides pizza. Afterwards they went into the family room so Austin could open his gifts, which included some from his parents, siblings, and out-of-town relatives, one from her family, and one from her. He saved hers for last, and she knew he would like what she had chosen. He had only mentioned the new album from his favorite group ten times in the last two weeks.

She had gotten him something else too, but she wanted to wait until later to give it to him. When she told him that while they were waiting for the candles to be lit on his birthday cake, he said, "You already got me two things."

"Two?" she asked.

"The CD and your picture."

She had forgotten about that until now and knew he must have gotten it in the mail today before they had picked him up to go watch Steven. He hadn't said anything about it before.

"Thank you, by the way," he said. "That's a nice picture of you, and what you wrote was good to hear. I think that night changed me a lot too, and I couldn't believe what you wrote about seeing each other face to face. That was too weird."

She didn't understand what he meant at first, but then she remembered the song. "Oh, yeah," she agreed. "I did say that, didn't I? That's funny."

"But I know what you mean," he said. "I'd like to think if you moved we would be able to write to each other like you and Sarah do, but I'm not sure that's possible. I'd much rather have you here."

They went into the dining room again so he could blow out his candles. He closed his eyes and made a wish before putting out all fourteen in one breath. When she asked him what he had wished for, he said, "Something I want to come true, so I'm not telling."

They each got their own plate of ice cream and cake. Austin had wanted to watch a movie as a part of his party, so they did that afterwards, and it was getting late by the time it was over, but she still insisted on him playing the song before she left.

They went to his room because he didn't want to sing it in front of everybody, and she saw her picture along with the letter on his desk. She picked up the photo for a moment and looked at it, realizing how much she had changed since it was taken. Her hair was longer now, and she had grown another inch taller. She couldn't tell that in the picture so much, but her face had a different look to it. She tried to imagine what she would look like in another two or three years, but she couldn't.

Austin looked different now too. He had gotten taller, had his braces now, and his hair had lightened over the summer. She had always thought he was cute, but he was growing into it more and more.

Austin sang the song through a couple of times, and she joined him on the melody once she got the sound of it in her head. It was simple, and she liked it. She thought about the truth of the lyrics once again, and she asked him something after he stopped playing.

"How have you seen Him face to face lately?"

"In the usual ways, I guess. I've just been thinking about it more."

"What usual ways?"

He shrugged. "How He takes care of us and brings good things into our lives. My family. The new building being finished. You."

"I see Him in our friendship too," she said. "It was fun having the whole day with you today. I got used to that last year at school, and I miss it."

"I guess we'll have to plan more times like this."

She smiled at him and had a strong desire to kiss him. She couldn't imagine what they would look like when they were seventeen, but she could imagine them being that age and kissing. She could imagine it as plain as day.

"So what about my other gift?" he said. "Do I get to see it now, or did you do something goofy like write a song for me?"

She laughed. "No, it's a real, hold in your hand kind of gift."

They went out to where she had left her coat and bag, and she took the wrapped package out of it. Handing it to him in the front hallway, she waited for him to tear off the paper and open the box, and he looked at the framed picture for a long time. It was one Sarah had taken of her and Austin together at camp, and she had put it in a frame that had the words 'Best Friends' written all around the edge. She was a little worried he might think it was too girlie of a gift, but his words and actions didn't indicate that.

Stepping forward and giving her a hug, he thanked her and said he loved it.

"I love you, Austin," she said easily. "I hope you can put a new picture of us in there every year."

"Me too," he said.

He released her and stepped back, but he was much closer to her than he had been before. "I should probably take you home now," he said and made a little joke. "Oh, but that's right, I can't get my license for two more years."

She laughed. "That's true. Maybe you should get your dad and tell him I'm ready to go home now."

"Yeah, I guess," he said. "Unless you want to sleep over."

She laughed again. "I don't think my dad would go for it, but that's nice of you to offer."

He stepped away and went to get his dad. She stepped into the family room to tell his mom good night and thanked them for inviting her. Mrs. Lockhart came over to give her a hug while Pastor Doug was getting his keys and Austin went to put his gift away before they left.

"I'm glad you could come," Mrs. Lockhart said. "I was surprised when Austin said he didn't want a Pizza Playhouse party this year, but not that surprised when he wanted to invite you here."

Brianne hadn't known this had been mainly Austin's idea, but she wasn't surprised. They left as soon as Austin returned. Pastor Doug had gotten a new truck recently, but otherwise the ride home had a similar feel as times they had done this before. The three of them talked about the building dedication next week, and Pastor Doug said he thought he would have them sing the song at the end because it related to what he planned to talk about.

When they got to the house, he told her good night, and she got out of the truck with Austin. He didn't linger once they reached the door, but she gave him another brief hug and told him 'Happy Birthday' before opening the door.

"Brianne?" he said before she was fully inside.

She turned back. "What?"

"I love you too."

She smiled. "I know you do."

"Good night."

"Good night, Austin. See you tomorrow."

She went inside. Her dad was doing the usual: going over his sermon notes for tomorrow's message, and her mom was relaxing on the couch, but she looked a little subdued, Brianne thought. They asked her about the evening, and she told them the basics, along with telling them about the song Austin wrote and her singing it with Danielle next week.

"Yes, she was over here earlier and told us about it," her mom said, flipping off the television with the remote and laying it on the coffee table.

"Oh? Why was she here?"

"I called and asked her to come. I got a call from Aunt Julie tonight. Jenna ran away, and I thought Danielle might be able to help with knowing where to look for her and the best way for Phil and Julie to handle this."

Brianne felt numb. Jenna was the same age as her. She couldn't imagine running away at thirteen. Where would she go?

"Did they find her?"

"Not yet. They know she's with one of her friends because she left them a note saying so, but all the friends they tried either don't know where she is or are lying about it."

"Why did she run away? Just because they won't let her date yet?"

"Yeah, that's part of it. She feels like they're being too restrictive, and then when she breaks the rules, she gets grounded, and that makes it worse. She was supposed to be grounded this weekend, and they think that's why she didn't come home on Friday after school. They're hoping she comes back by tomorrow night, and Danielle said she did that a lot—running away for the weekend, but they're still very worried, of course."

Brianne hugged her mom, feeling concerned for her cousin, but also as a way of reminding herself she was a part of a loving family she had no need or desire to run away from. And she didn't understand where Jenna's head was because she knew she had the same. Her parents were just trying to protect her. Why didn't she get that?

"I love you, Mom," she said. "I'm sorry this is happening."

"I love you too, baby."

She crossed the room to hug her dad also and then she asked if she could call Austin. He had been praying for Jenna too, and she didn't want to wait until tomorrow to let him know.

"Sure, honey," her dad said. "But not too long. I don't want Doug and Carrie thinking I let my daughter call boys at all hours of the night."

She smiled and went to make the call, supposing Austin would be home by now, and he was.

"Miss me already?" he said.

"No, well yes, but that's not why I'm calling."

"What's up?"

She told him, and he listened without comment until she was finished. "I'd appreciate it if you could pray for her. That's why I wanted to call instead of waiting until tomorrow."

"I will," he said. "And I'll pray for you too."

"Thanks. I feel more helpless with this than I ever did with Ashlee. At least Ashlee is here to try and be a positive influence on. But with Jenna, all I can do is pray."

"I'm sure that's enough," he said. "You're limited in what you can do, but God isn't. Don't forget that."

Chapter Fourteen

Brianne heard the phone ring when she was brushing her teeth, and she went out of the bathroom and down the hall with the toothbrush still in her mouth. Her mom had answered it, and she could tell by her mom's end of the conversation they had either found Jenna or she had come home on her own.

Spitting out the toothpaste in the kitchen sink, Brianne waited for her mom to reveal the news to her and her dad, who had both come into the room.

"She's home," her mom said. "She came home a few minutes ago and went to her room without telling them anything, but Julie wanted to let us know she's there at least."

Brianne felt like calling Austin back and saying, 'Wow, that's some fast connection you've got going with Jesus!', but she decided she'd better not press her luck with getting her mom and dad to agree to her making late-night calls, and she felt too relieved to joke about it anyway.

She hugged her mom and dad and went to the bathroom to put her toothbrush back before going to her room to go to bed. She'd had a fun day but felt tired, and she fell asleep easily.

In the morning she got ready for church and had a mostly normal Sunday. She told Austin about Jenna coming home shortly after she had called him, and he smiled.

"Well, it was my birthday. I think there's a special line for that."

She talked with Danielle about it that afternoon too, and Danielle agreed with Austin there wasn't much she could do except pray. "When I was messed up, I mostly only listened to who I considered to be my friends at the time and shut everyone else out. Trust God to reach her at the right time. It's a shame, but some of us really do have to learn things the hard way."

Danielle picked up the song quickly that Austin wrote, and she really liked it, just like Brianne knew she would. Brianne thought they sounded good together when they sang and Austin played the guitar, but Danielle was definitely the strongest element, and she rose to the occasion.

Anna and Josh were there. They had come to talk with Pastor Doug about some things for next Sunday, and he was meeting with them right after band rehearsal, but they listened to them practice first, and Anna thought they would be the highlight of the dedication. Brianne felt honored to be a part of something special like this, but she felt most glad the three of them were living the reality of the song, not just singing the words.

Danielle gave her a ride home like she often did, and although Danielle had told Austin how much she liked the song, she elaborated on that more to her privately.

"I can't believe Austin wrote that. What kind of fourteen-year-old guy writes a song like that?"

"Someone like Austin, I guess," Brianne laughed.

"I guess so. Has he written more, do you know?"

"Not that I know of," she said. "But I won't be surprised if that's the first of many."

"No kidding. Talk about hitting the target on the first try. I've tried writing tons of songs, but none of them have come close."

"Are you going to the concert on Thursday?" Brianne asked, changing the subject—in a way. "I love Bethany Dillon's music. I think you sound a lot like her."

"Thanks," Danielle said with a laugh. "But I can't write songs like her. And yes, I'm going. Is Sarah?"

"Yes, her youth group is coming too. We're going to try and find each other, but that might be tricky since it's all open seating."

"You could always call her," Danielle suggested. "She has a cell phone, doesn't she?"

"Yes, but I don't. I suppose I could borrow one."

"Yeah, like mine," she laughed.

Brianne appreciated the offer, and she knew she would probably do that. She had been trying to talk her parents into getting her a phone, but they didn't seem to think she had a need for it yet. And the truth was she didn't, but she wanted one. It seemed like everyone had one besides her.

"Is everything all right between you and Sarah?" Danielle asked.

"Yeah, sure," she said. "Why do you ask?"

"You got a little quiet there. I thought maybe something was wrong."

"No. I haven't seen her since we were at camp, but we had a great time, and we've been writing our usual weekly letters to each other. It will be good to see her at the concert though. I wasn't being quiet about that. I was thinking about not having a cell phone. I'm trying to be content without one, along with other things, but some days that's easier than others."

"You're not missing much," Danielle said. "I felt that way before I had one too, especially when we were living in California and all of my friends were getting them. The only reason my parents got me one was because they were concerned when I started not coming home like I should have. I was like, 'If I had a phone, I could call you, and then you wouldn't have to worry about me.' And so they did, but then I started lying about where I was. And if they tried to call me and I didn't want to answer, I'd lie and say I was at the movies where I'd had to turn it off."

Brianne knew some girls at school who did the same thing. "So, you're saying it's better to be home at a certain time than to have a phone so I can change my plans?"

"Definitely. It's amazing how fast we can get ourselves into trouble. I remember doing and saying things I never imagined until I was."

They had reached her house, and Danielle had driven all the way down her driveway because it was raining. Brianne undid her seat belt, and Danielle surprised her by leaning over and giving her a hug before she opened the door.

"Stay safe, Brianne," she said. "Let your mom and dad protect you. If I had done that, I never would have ended up in the pit."

"Okay," she said. "Thanks."

She got out of the car and went into the house. After telling her mom how rehearsal had gone, she went into the kitchen to call Sarah. It had been three weeks since she had talked to her. She told Sarah about Danielle's idea for them to call each other at the concert, and Sarah had something to ask her.

"Are you still planning to spend the weekend with me?"

Brianne hadn't told her about singing at the dedication next Sunday, and she had forgotten their original plan. They didn't have school on Friday, but the band was practicing on Saturday, and she and Danielle needed to go over the song a few more times.

"I'd love to, but I can't actually." She went on to tell her why and asked if she might like to come here instead. "I'll have to ask first, but do you think you could?"

"Probably," Sarah said. "How about if we both do that and then I'll call you back?"

"Okay."

"What song are you singing with Danielle?" Sarah asked.

"It's one Austin wrote."

"Austin?"

"Yes, it's really good! You have to come so you can hear it."

"Why am I getting the feeling it was a mistake for me to not pick him when I had the chance?"

"You move, you lose," she said, laughing at her own boldness of saying that.

"I guess so," Sarah said. "By the way, I have something to tell you on that subject—moving, I mean, but I'll wait until I call you back."

"Okay."

Brianne hung up the phone and went to talk to her mom about Sarah coming next weekend. Her mom said it would be fine as long as her mom and dad could come pick her up on Sunday because they were going to be busy with the dedication.

While Brianne waited for Sarah to call back, she wondered what Sarah had meant about telling her something on the subject of moving. Were they moving back? That had always been a possibility. The reason Sarah's dad had been transferred was because of the cutbacks here, but she had tried to never get her hopes up.

She could feel them rising now, but she wondered what that would be like. Would their friendship go back to being the way it was, or would it be different because she had so many other friends? And what would happen to her relationship with Austin if Sarah was living here again? She had mixed feelings.

When Sarah called back, she said she could come next weekend, and Brianne was excited about it. Sarah's parents could pick her up on Sunday, and they were going to come for the dedication too because they'd had a part in the original decision to take on the project.

"So, what's this about moving?" Brianne reminded her after they discussed the details of next weekend. "Are you moving back?"

"No," Sarah said. "I wish, but this is good too."

"What?"

"It's not for sure, but it looks like my dad is going to get a promotion after the first of the year. Something he deserved five years ago, but it wasn't available then."

"But if he gets it, you'll have to move again?"

"Yes. To Eugene. That's where the opening is."

"Eugene? That's another two hours away."

"I know. That's a bummer, but otherwise it will be a good thing. My mom won't have to work full-time anymore, and the job will be easier on my dad."

"Are you upset about moving away from your friends there?"

"Not as much as moving away from you. I'll miss Ryan and Briana, but—I'll be okay."

"At least that's close to the camp," Brianne said. "We can still meet there in the summer and maybe when my family goes down to visit the Wests."

"Yeah, I was thinking that."

"When will you know for sure?"

"In another week or two. Maybe by next weekend."

They talked for awhile longer without running out of things to say, and Brianne told her about Austin's birthday and how fun that had been.

"Sounds like a sneaky way for Austin to get a date with you, if you ask me," Sarah teased her, and Brianne didn't deny it. She told her about the pictures she had given Austin, the framed one of them together and the other one.

"I thought about suggesting it when I sent you that picture," Sarah said, "but I didn't want to talk you into something you weren't comfortable with."

Brianne laughed. "I thought of that as soon as I saw it. And I was a little nervous beforehand, but when I gave it to him, it was fine. He really is my best friend, and that amazes me. We don't work at it, it just happens."

"That's the best kind," Sarah said.

"I know, just like me and you."

"Yep. Even when we're not living next door to each other."

"Or when me and Austin don't have all of our classes together. It's still the same anyway."

"It think that's a part of eternity," Sarah said.

"What do you mean?"

"Like, eternity isn't just about things going on forever, but also about the special people in our lives and the special moments always being with us, even when the actual time has passed."

"Like me and you not having to start over every time we see each other?"

"Yeah."

"I agree," she said, "but I'm still glad you're coming next weekend."

"Me too. I won't have to share you like I did at camp. At least not all the time."

After letting Sarah go, Brianne decided to call Austin and tell him about their plans. He wasn't too surprised Sarah was coming and said he would try to stay out of their way, but he did suggest the three of them doing something together on Friday in the afternoon, like going to the movies, and she thought that would be fun.

"Have you heard anything more about your cousin?"

"My aunt called earlier today and gave my mom more details, but it's hard to know how much of what Jenna is saying is the truth. She claims to have been at her friend's house the whole time, but who knows?"

"I was thinking last night about how close I could have come to that. A year and a half ago I thought I wanted to be anyplace but living in this house, but now this is my favorite place to be."

"What changed that?" she asked, sort of having an idea but wanting to hear his perspective on it.

"A lot of things, but mostly you."

That wasn't what she expected him to say. "Me? Don't you mean God?"

"Yeah, but He got my attention through you. I've told you that."

"I know, but it's not about me. It's about what He showed you through me."

"It's both," he said. "Jesus and you."

She could accept that. She was who she was because of Jesus; but Sarah, Austin, her other friends, her family, and others were a part of it too.

Thinking of her family then, she knew she needed to spend some time with them after being gone all evening yesterday and being busy with church this morning and rehearsal this afternoon.

"I should go. I've been on the phone for almost an hour between you and Sarah, and I need to help J.T. with his book report. See you tomorrow?"

"I'll be there."

She did spend the rest of the day with her family, and they watched one of their favorite movies together before her younger siblings had to be in bed.

Afterwards, her mom and dad talked to her about their plans for Thanksgiving they had come up with last night. They had decided it would be good to go up to Bellingham sooner rather than waiting until Christmas. Her mom wanted to have some time with Aunt Julie then, and her aunt and uncle had asked her dad to talk to Jenna while they were up there. Not just as a concerned uncle, but as a pastor they were hoping she would listen to better than her own.

"Do you want to go too?" they surprised her by asking. "If you think it would be too difficult for you to be there, you could spend the weekend with Sarah or the Wests. We'll probably go back at Christmas too."

She was tempted to take them up on that. She would love to see either Sarah or Joel, and spending the weekend with one of her close friends would be far easier and more pleasant than seeing Jenna and Justine after what had happened last year.

But they were her cousins, and she cared about them, and she didn't like the thought of what kind of silent message she would be sending if she didn't come for Thanksgiving. If her whole family wasn't going, that

would be one thing, but her choosing to be elsewhere—
that didn't settle well with her spirit.

"No, I'll go," she said. In a flash of inspiration she added, "Can I invite Austin to go with us?"

Her dad stared at her, and her mom smiled and then laughed.

"What makes you ask that?" he said.

"I think it would be good for Jenna to see me with one of my friends."

"Why not Sarah?"

She thought about that. "I think her seeing me with Sarah would make her mad. She would be jealous of our friendship. But with Austin, I think she would be curious. And Austin can be really blunt and honest with people without being mean about it, you know? Like he does with Ashlee. They used to fight all the time, but not so much anymore. He's worn down that tough exterior of hers."

Brianne was secretly shocked when her parents actually agreed to let her ask Austin. They wanted to make sure it was okay with his mom and dad first, and she wanted to think and pray about it a little more before she asked him, but for now she thought it could be a good thing, and she suspected Jesus had given her the idea in the first place.

Chapter Fifteen

On Thursday after school, Brianne went home on the bus but was meeting up with Austin and her other friends an hour later at the church. Because they didn't have school tomorrow, and because they didn't go to concerts very often as a youth group, they had a big crowd going that consisted of both those who were older than her and younger. Brianne had a good feeling in her heart about what the evening would hold for all of them, and for what her time with Sarah this weekend would be like.

Ever since being at camp and talking with Austin about it, she knew being a part of this group and seeing others around her coming face to face with Jesus was something that brought her a lot of joy. But she couldn't force it and try to make it happen herself. She needed to focus on her own relationship with God, keeping it as real as possible, and letting others see that. It was mostly a matter of watching Jesus work—sometimes through things she said or did, and other times through someone else, like Austin or Pastor Doug or Anna.

Tonight it would likely be through Bethany, the singer-songwriter they were going to see. And she had a confident feeling in her heart about it.

"What's that smile for?" Austin said, coming to stand beside her as they waited for everyone to arrive.

She told him, and he took her words seriously, and he reminded her of them later when they saw several in their group respond to the message that was given. Marissa's brother Miguel had come to know Jesus and been baptized last spring, but his girlfriend, Andrea, was still skeptical. She came to youth group on a regular basis, but the truth didn't sink in for her. But tonight it did, and she was crying in a way Brianne had never seen anyone cry over allowing God to reach her heart.

Ashlee and Caitlin were there too, along with their friend Jillene, and all three of them were deeply touched by something Bethany said. Brianne wasn't sure what exactly, but she didn't need to know. She just prayed it would go beyond tonight and make a difference for them in their lives back home.

There were some others Brianne didn't know as well who seemed to take God in a more personal way, including some of their faithful high schoolers who were there every week and very involved in the ministry-end of things, and Brianne couldn't help but think it was perfect timing with the dedication coming up on Sunday.

Afterwards Brianne, Austin, and Sarah went outside the large church to wait for the others to come out. Pastor Doug and Anna and Josh were still inside with those who had stayed after the concert to pray or talk with friends or counselors who were there. And even though Sarah's youth group was here, she had chosen to sit with them, and the three of them formed a little huddle where none of them spoke or prayed out loud, but Brianne knew the two of them could feel it too.

This was a holy, sacred moment for several people they knew, and somehow they were a part of it. Danielle and Silas joined them after a few minutes, and the five of them stood there silently with their arms linked. Brianne had been touched by the music also. It had given her an overall sense of hope and that she was loved deeply by her God. No matter what came at her now, it was all going to be okay.

"I heard you wrote a song, Austin," Sarah said, being the one to break the silence. "Maybe in another five years we'll all be going to see you in concert."

"I can't sing, but I might be writing songs and playing back-up for these two," he said, pointing to her and Danielle.

"You can sing," Brianne said.

"Not like you two sing."

"I can't wait to hear it," Sarah said. "Have you, Silas?"

"No, not yet," he said. "Maybe they could sing it for us now."

"I don't have my guitar," Austin said.

"And we don't have the words," Danielle added. "Sorry, you'll have to wait until Sunday."

Brianne didn't want to sing it by herself without Austin playing the guitar, but she knew the words well enough by heart. She had looked over them several times this week and had been humming the notes and words to herself often.

"What's the name of it?" Sarah asked.

"Face To Face," Austin answered. "It's about coming face to face with God for who He really is."

"Austin!" Sarah laughed. "Who are you? I'm gone for a year, and you turn into this?"

He laughed. "You've seen me plenty. I hope this isn't the first time you've noticed any change since last summer."

"Change, yes! But this? This is beyond change. This is—I don't even know. You're fourteen, and you're writing songs like Jeremy Camp?"

"I wouldn't go that far," Austin said. "But I'm sure Jeremy had to start sometime. I feel like, 'I'm fourteen, and this is the first song I've ever written about God? What's my problem?'"

"You're in good company," she said. "And if you become famous someday, we can all say 'We knew him when—'"

"Okay, my first concert," Austin played along. "You're all invited. I'll get you seats in the front row, I promise."

Brianne laughed along with the others, but she believed Austin had the potential for such a thing. When she had first met him three years ago, he'd been nice but mostly quiet. But he wasn't anymore. Fourteen or not, he was the most popular member of the youth group—even more so than some of the high school guys, and yet he wasn't arrogant about it or using his place as the youth pastor's son to have special privileges like playing the drums or doing a special music performance for the youth building dedication on Sunday. He had earned it.

He was the real thing. A real friend. A real follower of Jesus. A real musician with gifts he was using the way God led him to. A real teenager with hopes and dreams for the future.

On the way back to the vans, Sarah was talking with Danielle and Silas, and she and Austin fell behind. Brianne didn't realize she was looking at Austin in a unique way until he said something.

"What?"

She was already looking at him, and she smiled. "What, what?"

"You're looking at me weird," he said. "Do I have mustard on my nose or something?"

"No," she laughed, linking arms with him. "I was thinking about what you said back there, about being a famous musician someday."

"Somehow I doubt that, but thanks for the vote of confidence."

"What makes you doubt it?"

"Writing one song and becoming famous for it are googles of miles apart."

"But like you said, everyone has to start somewhere."

"That's true, but there's a lot more people who are musically gifted who aren't famous than those who are."

"Is that what you want to do with your life, something with music?"

"I have no idea," he said. "Right now I enjoy playing drums and learning guitar. Maybe I'll still be interested ten years from now, or maybe I won't. Dreams can be a good thing, but I think we can get too far ahead of ourselves sometimes. Right now I just want to be fourteen and enjoy it."

"Are you?"

He smiled. "I've got you for a best friend; of course I'm enjoying it."

Brianne had a fun time with Sarah the following day. They had both gotten off to a good start for their eighth-grade year, and they had a lot to talk about. They also enjoyed doing the things they used to when Sarah lived next door, like scrapbooking, watching their favorite movies, doing homework together, and listening to music while painting their nails and playing card games. In addition to their old favorites, Briana had taught Sarah a couple of new ones, and they were really fun too.

On Saturday afternoon they had worship band rehearsal, and Sarah came along to listen. Afterwards she and Danielle and Austin went through the song, and Brianne felt nervous about tomorrow, but she knew the song well. Pastor Doug offered to take the four of them out for pizza, but Danielle had to go home because one of her friends was coming over, so Pastor Doug got pizza to take home and invited her and Sarah to come, and they spent part of the evening with Austin's family.

Sarah told them about possibly moving. Brianne hadn't said anything about it to Austin or anyone yet because they didn't know for sure. She had been hoping Sarah would know by this weekend, but her dad wouldn't get the final word until later next week.

In the morning, they had a shortened Sunday morning service, followed by a potluck brunch, and then the dedication ceremony was after that. The youth band played, and Pastor Doug said some good things about his vision for the future of the youth ministry and the use of the building, and then she and Danielle sang the song, and Brianne had a unique feeling. She sang with Danielle all the time, and Austin was on stage with them every week, but it was different.

She wasn't sure if it was because Austin was playing guitar, it was a performance rather than leading others in worship, or because of the song itself, but she came away with a kind of joy she wasn't sure she had ever experienced. Not pride for how good it sounded, but simply a joy of being a part of it.

Sarah had to leave shortly after that, and she told her good-bye in the parking lot beside the car. Sarah said she would let her know about her dad's job and also asked if she wanted to come visit for her birthday weekend again this year, and Brianne knew she would do that if possible, especially if Sarah was going to be moving in January.

After she was gone, Austin was waiting for her outside the front door of the new building, and Brianne was anxious to get back inside because it was so cold out today, but Austin held her back.

"Why didn't you tell me Sarah might be moving?"

"They don't know for sure."

"How are you feeling about it?"

She shrugged. "I don't know. I know it's a good thing for her family, but I probably won't see her as much as I've been able to for the past year."

He gave her a hug, seeming to know this was a bigger deal than she was allowing herself to think about right now. "Great job on the song," he said, changing the subject.

She'd heard that from a lot of others but not him yet. "Thanks for writing a great song," she said, stepping back and saying something she hadn't said to anyone else. "I've been thinking about the words all week, and they've reminded me of what this is all about."

"Yeah, me too," he said. "I started out thinking I was writing a song for God, but I think He really wrote it for me."

"And me," she added, realizing that's what had given her a unique feeling while they were singing. She often thought of singing as something she did for God, but it was for her too. Singing about the truth of God's love and goodness and what He wanted for her was a weekly reminder of it all. And for as long as she lived, she doubted she would ever forget that song.

She hadn't had a chance to ask Austin about going with her family to Bellingham over Thanksgiving, and she'd had it in her mind to ask him sometime today, so she decided this was a good time. First she told him they were going and why, and about her parents' offer to let her stay with Sarah or the Wests, but why she had decided against it.

"I do want to see Jenna and Justine, and I'm praying about an opportunity to talk with Jenna, but I think it would be good if she could see me with one of my friends. She has one idea in her mind about what it's like to be a teenager, and I think we could show her a different way.

"We?"

"Yeah, you and me. Do you want to go?"

He stared at her. "Have you talked to your mom and dad about this?"

"Yes. And they've talked to your mom and dad. It's okay with them, but I only want you to go if you really want to. If you think it's a stupid idea, or you don't want to, just say so."

They were interrupted by some people coming out of the building. It was an older couple who had been a part of this church for a long time and were very supportive of the youth program. Mrs. Gardner gave them both a hug and told them how great the song had sounded, and Mr. Gardner echoed his wife's words and shook their hands. By the time they stepped away, others were coming outside also, and Austin pulled her away before anyone else could spot them.

"It's cold out here, let's go inside," he said, leading her to a side door and stepping into the hallway with classrooms on either side. Those who were still here were in the main room where the dedication ceremony had taken place.

Brianne waited for him to respond to her suggestion, fully expecting he might say no or he wanted to think about it. But he couldn't resist teasing her before he gave her an answer.

"If I go, will I get to meet Alex?"

She hadn't been thinking about seeing him, let alone Austin meeting him and sizing up his competition, and she laughed. "Probably. He did want to take me out somewhere. I might go if you tagged along."

"No, no. I don't want to chaperone your first date. I want to be your first date."

"Well, I'm still only thirteen, so let's focus on next month. Do you want to go?"

"Yes."

"Really?"

"Mmmm, let's think about this...four days away from my best friend, or four days with her? Yeah, that's a tough one."

She smiled and didn't feel surprised by his response, but she felt like this was completely crazy. What made him want to be around her so much? What did she possibly have to offer him? He couldn't date her. He couldn't kiss her. He couldn't even hold her hand or call her his girlfriend. And if one day she said, 'Okay, I changed my mind. You can do all that,' he wouldn't let her. He would tell her to be true to herself and what she really wanted.

"You're crazy, Austin Lockhart," she said, stepping forward to give him a hug. "Completely crazy."

"Not that crazy, Brianne. Other than my family, you're the best thing in my life. Didn't I make that clear when you were the only person I invited to my birthday party?"

"Yes," she replied. "I just don't get why."

He stepped back and laughed. "Why?"

"Yeah. You have lots of friends. Everyone likes you. Why me?"

Chapter Sixteen

Austin sat against the wall and pulled her down with him. Sitting there beside her, face to face and holding her hand in his, Austin began to list the reasons why he liked her best.

"You don't get on my nerves—ever; most people do at least some of the time. Even Sarah was being a little too "sweet" this weekend. You know what I mean?"

She knew what he meant. Sarah wasn't that way with her, but she acted a little different around Austin. "And? That's it? I don't get on your nerves?"

"No, that's the result of a bunch of other stuff. You like to goof around and have fun, but you're not stupid about it. You like to tease, but you don't embarrass me. You never lead me into making bad choices. You help me with my homework without making me feel stupid. You could have me as your boyfriend, but you know we're not ready for that, so you put everything you have to give into our friendship instead. And you're always yourself. I never feel like you're one person one day and someone different the next."

Brianne knew she didn't do anything except be herself and enjoy Austin for who he was too. He didn't make her mad. He didn't ignore her. He was fun to be with, and she never felt uncomfortable around him. He didn't lead her to do the wrong things either, and he was always there for whatever she needed.

"Sometimes I feel stupid for making us wait," she said.

"Don't, Brianne. It's not stupid. It's smart."

She knew he was right, but she was completely honest with him on that subject. "Sometimes I don't want to wait."

He smiled. "Yes, you do. You just don't feel like it sometimes. There's a difference."

"I'm scared of losing you, Austin," she whispered.

He touched her face and spoke without any hesitation. "You're not losing me. At least not for that reason. I will never choose someone else because I'm tired of waiting for you."

"I'm afraid of hurting you. Of making you wait and then—"

"That won't hurt me, Brianne. Maybe we're waiting for each other, or maybe we're helping each other wait for other people. Either way, we'll both be the better for it."

Since his birthday, she had been having some strong desires for him to kiss her whenever they were together, especially if they were face to face like they were now. But his words made that desire flee. She had thought that before too, but she needed him to remind her of it, and he had.

"I loved singing that song today," she said. "I liked us doing something like that together."

"Me too. I liked hearing you sing something I wrote."

"I want us to help each other live it."

"I don't know about that," he said. "Maybe when we're sixteen we can get serious about this God-stuff, but now? Come on."

"I think it's too late. I don't think I can let go now."

"Of me?"

She laughed. "No."

"Oh, I forgot one. You always laugh at my lame jokes."

"And you always make me laugh."

"That's because I like seeing you happy."

"Don't change the subject. We were talking about staying face to face with Jesus. How do you think we can help each other do that?"

"No clue," he said. "I forgot one more."

"What?" she laughed.

"You're beautiful."

"And you are changing the subject," she said, feeling secretly thrilled he would say that—especially since Sarah had been here all weekend and she had felt some of those insecurities about herself rising more than once.

"Is Alex cuter than me?"

"You'll find out next month."

"He's cuter, just say it."

"He's cuter," she said. "Now back to—"

"How is he cuter?" Austin demanded.

She started laughing and couldn't stop. Austin had this completely adorable side to him that he didn't let many people see. Not even her until this summer, and she hadn't seen it very often.

"Okay, I give up trying to have a serious conversation with you. Let's go help your dad like we promised. Most people are gone now."

"I know how," he said, turning serious before she could get up.

She leaned back against the wall. "Seriously?"

"Seriously."

"How?"

"We keep a close eye on each other, looking for anything out of the ordinary. We know each other well enough to notice when we're not being real with each other or those around us. And I think that goes together with when we're not being real with God, don't you?"

"Yes," she said. "Like if you're being a jerk, or I'm being overly sensitive, there's a reason behind it."

"Or if we're too busy for each other or for our families, then we're probably too busy for God too, and we can call each other on that."

"Or if our friendship isn't working anymore."

"Or if one day I try to kiss you. That's probably more about something being missing in another part of my life."

"Is it okay if I let you kiss me before I tell you that?"

He tickled her, and she squealed and jumped to her feet. He came after her, and they entered the main room laughing and catching the attention of others, namely her mom and dad who were taking tablecloths off the tables that had been set up in the gymnasium-like room. It had a stage on one end, basketball hoops, and classrooms and office-space along the side.

"I thought that was a long time for you to be saying good-bye to Sarah," her dad said.

"Sorry, we were having a very spiritual conversation."

"Yeah, I can see that," he laughed. "I think Pastor Doug needs your help in the kitchen."

"Okay," she said, crossing the room to where a full-sized kitchen was located on the other end of the building, not blaming her dad for not believing their excuse, even if it was true.

They helped Pastor Doug with cleaning up from the brunch, along with Anna and Josh. While she was washing dishes with Anna, her youth leader mentioned something she was thinking of doing next month. Anna wanted to have a girls' slumber party at her house one Friday night, and Brianne thought that sounded like fun.

"I thought maybe we could have pizza for dinner at the house, then go bowling or something, and come back to the house for a movie before we go to bed."

"That would be great," she said. "May I make one request?"

"Sure."

"Can we not play Truth or Dare, or any other embarrassing games?"

"Definitely," Anna said. "I want everyone to have fun, but I have better games we can play than that."

"Can we invite friends?"

"Absolutely."

Brianne felt like telling Anna about seeing her cousins again on Thanksgiving, so she did, and she asked her to pray for her and for any advice she had to share.

"I think you have to wait for the right opportunities to say something, but I also think God will give you those opportunities if you ask Him for them and you really have something worthwhile to say. I prayed for Janie, Josh's sister, for a lot of years before that opportunity ever came, but it did, and it came at just the right time."

"How is she doing?"

"Good," Anna said. "It seems like she gets a little better every day, and she's talking about getting involved in helping out with youth group too. I think that would be a good move for her, but only when she feels ready. She really liked your song today. She had to leave because Michael needed a nap, but she wanted me to tell you that."

"Thanks," Brianne said. "I enjoyed singing it. I told Austin he has to write more."

"I agree," Anna said. "And if you're the one singing them, I'm sure he'll be more than happy to do that."

Brianne didn't comment, but she hoped Anna was right. She knew whatever words Austin had to write would be coming from another heart like hers: A heart that believed in God's love for her and wanted to love Him back with all of her heart, soul, mind, and strength. A heart that wanted to keep meeting her God face to face.

Humming the song as she dried the remaining dishes and put them away, she not only thought about the words but had a moment with Jesus right there in the midst of her work, and she had no doubt the words would be answered in many ways in the days, weeks, and months to come.

What I want, Jesus
Is to see you face to face
Maybe that won't be
Until I enter Heaven
Or maybe I can see you today

I love to hear from my readers

Write me at:

living_loved@yahoo.com

Made in the USA
Coppell, TX
27 July 2020

31837090R00095